48

8

BLITZ

48 BLITZ

BRETT BIEBEL

SPLIT LIP PRESS

Published by Split/Lip Press
6710 S. 87th St.
Ralston, NE 68127
www.splitlippress.com

ISBN: 9781952897047

Cover Design by David Wojciechowski

Editing by Pedro Ramírez

"The only thing very noticeable about Nebraska was that it was still, all day long, Nebraska."

—Willa Cather

For Meg

Table of Contents

1st

Quarter

Big Red Nation

The state of Nebraska executed Matthew Alan Nowinski at 10:47 AM on a Friday, some 32 hours before the biggest Husker football game in at least a decade. In fact, in the days leading up to the execution, some 200 or so citizens had written to the governor asking for a stay, and most of these letters said basically the same thing. Nowinski was a fan. I support the death penalty. We don't want the bad karma. What's the harm in waiting a few days, or, better yet, until the season's over? If he's gonna go anyway, surely a month or two either way doesn't matter, and doesn't this happen all the time?

For his part, the governor conferenced with staff that morning, and at least one advisor urged him to just issue the stay. After all, the letters were right. Nowinski would be dead no matter what. Why risk angering a couple hundred diehards and maybe losing some votes when we could just as easily say it's about reconfirming a few details or because our fentanyl supplier fell through or any number of other procedural reasons, this advisor argued, and the governor himself appeared to consider it. Then someone else piped up and said there was no way a couple hundred Husker fans who supported the death penalty were ever gonna vote for a Democrat, and you know how conspiratorial everyone is these days. We delay and give a bogus reason, the press is sure to come sniffing around. And, if we're honest, if we say we're worried about bad karma, then isn't that like saying the death penalty's something we should be ashamed of when we all know it's nothing if not the truest and purest form of justice we got? Not to mention biblically sanctioned, and if we frame it as an act of mercy, well, then we look like bleeding hearts, don't we, and remember what they did to Dukakis? Too much risk, not enough reward, she said.

Ultimately, the latter argument won out. A small group of protestors gathered outside the state prison in Lincoln, most of them Catholic nuns who didn't care much about football (although there was one, Sister Perpetua William, who pinned a big red N to her jacket and talked to one of the journalists about the days of Tom Osborne and Tommie Frazier, and how, if she wore the big hat, one of them would be the real St. Thomas and the other beatified at the very least). They prayed for Nowinski. Read letters from some old friends talking up his generosity, how he used to buy drinks for the whole bar after touchdowns. Asked God to bring healing and peace to all touched by his crimes.

Inside the execution room, Nowinski knew very little about any of this and cared even less. He'd resigned himself to his fate years ago. He had Mulberry's for his last meal. Chatted with the guards about Ohio State being overrated and let it be known that, were he a betting man, he'd sure as hell take the points. When it came time for his last words, he gave a wave in the direction of his witnesses and said, "I love my Huskers, but they get their asses kicked tomorrow, no way I'll be sorry I missed it." Somebody laughed quietly. Then they brought out the needle, and everything went mostly as expected. Nowinski coughed a few times. At the very end, according to one of the media observers, he "turned the deepest red you ever saw," though exactly what kind of omen this was nobody could quite figure.

The Patron of the Prairie

They tell the story different ways in different places. Sometimes the farmer's name is Hobart, and sometimes it's Williams or Delacqua, but the underlying structure is always the same. He's got this chicken (or beef or turkey) operation. Family-run. Recently fallen on hard times. Treats his animals like kings but doesn't have time for all that organic certification bullshit and basically has to trick himself into thinking they get slaughtered the same way he does it at home (which, for chickens, is all individual and involves only the knife and a five-gallon plastic bucket) every time he sends a batch off to market. Now, pretty much everyone around Lincoln or Clay or Buffalo County or wherever has gone and contracted the whole business out to Tyson or Perdue or one of the other big ag producers because they can't make the ends meet any other way, and he's thought about it. Asked around. Had a neighbor tell him, "Listen, Bill [or Nick or Steven or Jerry], it's a real soul-crusher at first, but then you get used to it, and you can't beat the money neither." So, he goes to tour the guy's place, but as soon as he's within twenty feet of the coop he turns so red he swallows his Copenhagen and spends the drive back puking out the window of his truck. And then of course he gets home to find some asshole rep waiting in the driveway with paperwork because word travels fast, and it takes all he has not to clock the fucker (who, in one of the apocryphal versions, is from Cargill, and the story follows his POV for a while, through various hotels along I-80, nights spent breathing in chlorine and growing angrier by the minute until one day he's back in his own bed and wakes up soaked in sweat after dreaming about the Virgin Mary and decides to quit, to get divorced and just give up everything and move to some ranch in Wyoming that takes care of ex-race horses or troubled teens or something along those lines) after the third no.

So that night he's despondent. Wife catches him smoking for the first time in 20 years and says if the boys see they'll kill him much quicker than that cigarette, which gives the crafty bastard a burner of an idea. See, he don't have much, but he does have a family that's Husker through and through. Got a brother in the service and a father (or mother or sometimes it's a buddy from the corner bar) who's nothing if not practical. Gave him a life insurance policy for his 45th birthday. A big one. Quarter-, half-million, some reasonable fraction like that. He figures he's got maybe a year before the mortgage goes bust, and that's enough dough to get them out of debt and keep the operation moving without making him "morally compromised," as he puts it during a family meeting. At first, the wife and kids (who are maybe grown or else about to play their last couple years of high school football) are terrified, but then they figure there's no way he means it. They tell him to get some sleep. Crack a High Life. It ain't that bad, and we'll figure it out in the morning. They go to bed. He doesn't. There's too damn much to do.

It starts with the smoking. Packs a day. Winston Reds with coffee first thing and then four-egg omelets topped with enough cheese to embarrass a sewer rat. Lunch is McDonald's (or Mulberry's in some variations, and they'll for sure mention the "Heart Attack Platter," an actual meal the place still markets and serves in North Platte and Ogallala and pretty well up and down the interstate) or cheese curds topped with bacon and self-butchered chicken skin. He stops exercising. Gains 30 pounds. The family convinces itself it's depression or stress and will pass like wind through grass, though the wife gets worried enough she suggests a therapist even though she knows they can't pay for it and it'll be a waste of his time anyway. Sometimes he drives out to Walmart in the middle of the night because the fluorescence keeps him up, and the less he sleeps, the worse he figures he'll get. He pays for everything in cash. He burns the receipts. He spends hours reading about claims adjudication online and has friends go to the websites to print out documents because it can't be traceable to him, and the whole thing has to be done carefully to be done right, and no egghead adjuster is going to fuck up months of work. One day, seven, eight months in, it happens. There's constriction in his chest, and it starts getting hard to breathe. In some versions, it ends up being heartburn. Or diabetes. Sometimes he ignores the symptoms and tosses his phone and then changes his mind but can't make it back and dies next to a hen who gives him a peck or three before walking away. His wife finds him. He's saved. In Douglas County, he goes quick and quiet, but the real hero in that one is the insurance adjuster. He works for Mutual and sleuths out every fucking detail. There's a variation where the sons take the money, sell the farm to Tyson, and buy a condo in Kansas City and another where it works to perfection and no one ever finds out. But my own personal favorite is this one where the claim gets denied. The family keeps calling to argue even though they know it's hopeless, and just as they're out of cusses and tears and ready to exit the scene themselves, there's a bona fide miracle. The whole town, county, all of Nebraska is in their driveway. They've got envelopes with cash. There are notes that say "Free Silver" or "Huskers Do," and, for a minute, the whole thing feels like *It's a Wonderful Life*.

How to Live Forever

Then there's the version where the guy doesn't have life insurance at all. He's broke. Not an asset to his name. But, as luck would have it, he meets Warren Buffett at some bar in North Platte, and Buffett's three sheets to the wind. Just completely toasted on rum and Coca-Cola and running off at the mouth about everything. Baseball, politics, economic policy, Heinz ketchup, whatever you can imagine, and pretty soon he gets to talking about death. He tells the guy, listen, there's something I've always wanted to do, and I'd pay you handsomely because you seem like just the type. Now, naturally, this terrifies the guy. He starts to walk away, but Buffett grabs his elbow and says, I swear, it's nothing sexual or demeaning, and you don't have to do nothing, just hear me out. So, okay, the guy says, fine. Buy me another High Life, and let's talk. So, Buffett does. He says, Lot of people don't know this, but I got a libertarian streak in me, and you know where it comes out the most? No, says the guy. Funerals, says Buffett. Why, I was at one just the other day, some ConAgra exec overdosed on something, and I'd lay odds on Viagra, but you didn't hear it from me. Anyway, I'm sitting there thinking, you know, these places, they'll refuse to hold any kind of memorial without a death certificate. As in, like, they're legally required to have one, and what business does the state have in knowing you're dead? And this isn't some kind of death tax rant either because I'm more than happy to pay my fair share, but you're dead, and you still got to go and get someone to tell the government on your behalf? What bullshit is that? Post-mortem bureaucracy if you ask me, and what I want to do is give some guy a boatload of money. Just as much as he could spend in any one lifetime and buy him a nice plot of land out in the Panhandle. Somewhere between Kimball and Scottsbluff feels right, and this guy would be taken care of. Food, beer, women, cars, you name it, and it's all on me with just the one condition. When he dies, I got to be the first and only person to know. And then he's got to let me come over there and bury his body in the backyard. I'll do it at night. Dig the hole myself. No Bobcat, no third party, no nothing. Just a shovel and sweat under the stars. And there can't be a funeral, and no one can say goodbye, and everything has to be all under wraps and kept very tight. See, the whole point is no certificate. No loose ends. Nobody petitioning the state for death in abstentia, and nobody snooping around, and I'll buy out the whole county if I have to because it's got to be just, that's it. You're gone, and nobody knows. Which means you're still eligible to vote. The direct mail people are still sending you ads for televisions and light bulbs, and even some clerk from the future, he sees your name two centuries from now, he's got no idea when you checked out. You're not even dead, really. You're only presumed, and that's a big difference, and how about a toast to immortality, to the Sisyphean splendor of falling through the cracks? Buffet lifts his glass. The guy takes a minute, but eventually his comes up too, and this was fifteen years ago now, and they say nobody's heard so much as a rumor since.

The Fat Man

I once did a profile on a guy who called himself Ogallala Rolls. Every summer, from August 1ˢᵗ through the 10ᵗʰ, he'd park a 1986 Winnebago Chieftain near the shoulder of Exit 55 and set up a 20-foot-high cardboard cutout of an LGM-30 Minuteman III ICBM and a sign that would say something like "Ask me about my missile" in these big red letters. The year I was with him, there was also a picture of Ogallala (who, at the time, was 5' 11", 297 pounds) shirtless and in American flag sunglasses. He told me the photo was meant to "encourage gawking, rubbernecking, or the simple act of stopping to talk."

His mission was educational, he said. There were missiles buried out here, decaying maybe, dotting the prairie like land mines or snake holes, and people (namely travelers blowing on through at 85, 90 miles an hour), well, they needed to know. "You know what they get in New York? Everything we grow served up in nice, clean packages under bright lights and antiseptic smells. And here we are with the feedlots and slaughterhouses and goddamn instruments of death." We were in the kitchen when he said that. There were bananas on the counter that had to be half-fermented and a toaster I never saw him use. It was so humid you could barely breathe. Semis would hit potholes and rattle the whole RV, and Ogallala had a knack for telling what was being hauled just by the sound. Livestock, sometimes. Repossessed cars. Gasoline and prefab houses, all on their way somewhere else, somewhere "'better,'" like San Francisco, which "might as well be the end of the fucking world." Sometimes we'd hear a drawn-out honk, and Ogallala would raise his fist and rap the ceiling, as if the driver could hear.

I asked him maybe a hundred questions over the course of the ten days, most of them about things my editor thought people would want to know. How'd he get the cutout (buddy worked in a button factory outside of Chappell, and they snuck in at 2:00 AM with a case of High Life and told the overnighters to go find a ditch to enjoy it in) and what'd he eat (a nephew of his managed the Mulberry's down State 19 and would run us Weasel burgers and milkshakes twice a day) and didn't he get bored (seeing as the whole time I was there only one person, a woman who rode a motorcycle and had a Kansas City Royals tattoo on her neck, stopped to talk, and all she really wanted was a picture and directions to Carhenge, which Ogallala said was "across the River Styx"), which I knew was a stupid question after about five minutes because this was the kind of man content in his own company. Willing to sit on a lawn chair and listen to a ballgame while reading *Penthouse* and Pynchon, and if it wasn't for needing money that's what he'd have done all day. People could stop or they couldn't, and it was better if they did, but he wasn't crying out for entertainment, and if time ever did start to drip on by there was always the two jugs of corn mash under the sink inside, and it tasted strong enough to fuel the RV. I did ask him why he did it and what was the point, and that turned his eyes red and his voice shaky and elicited the answer that made my editor pull the plug on the story, which, in the end, was probably the right call. He said, "This is civil disobedience. This is a one-man revolution. And you've got these sons a bitches hiding out underground in Nevada and using computers to drop bombs on villages halfway across the world, and who's ever gonna call them to task? I been here trying to stir up some kind of confrontation since 2006, and I'd love to think I'd have the guts to knock out a sworn officer of the United States Air Force and then remove every last one of his teeth with a rusty pliers, but I'll settle for telling him he works for an asshole. That he's a goddamn imperialist and a good little German, and his mother must feel like shit for having birthed such a snot-nosed fascist fuck."

The Little Boy

There was no time to teach him all the secrets, to pass him the story quilt and watch that toddler face turn surprised and scared and proud. No time to formally grant first-generation status, first generation to grow up speaking English and first generation to go to college, even if it had to be a crumbling gray juco surrounded by prairie grass and wheat fields, with auto mechanics and grocery store clerks smoking cigarettes and maybe marijuana outside, alternating between a desire for that educational fresh start and the knowledge that it would never actually arrive. No time to teach him cynicism. Idealism. The way the sun hits the high plains and the highways start their climb to the West. No time for politics or ancestry, stories of U.S. loyalty in Laos and then a harried flight through mud and jungle, leaving behind great-uncles and cousins, maybe even a girl or two who could have been his mother, all casualties of the war against Asian communism. The proxy war. The Secret War. The war he'd never know about, the war that would always remain just a whisper. A past he managed to permanently escape.

His father was a custodian, a high school janitor who used to love the summers. Waking up at 4:00 AM and feeling the blast of fresh humidity outside, the silent, dark morning commute with the radio tuned to a country station. He used to let the old pickup run in the parking lot when he got to work, savoring every last second alone. Before the office. The dust. The clang of boiler pipes and gum stuck underneath hundreds of desks. Teachers who left crumbs on the floor, wrappers from Mulberry's and grease-stained pizza boxes, the football players tracking mud and grass through the halls and into the weight room by 9:00 AM. He scrubbed sweat and shit all day for $8.25 an hour, probably because he was too deferential to ask for a raise. Happy for the insurance. The uniform. A shy Christian kid or two who might actually stop him and say "thank you" as he swept around the remedial classroom, trying to learn a few new English words from a driving instructor or track coach who always spoke too fast. And they'd be gone by noon. And he'd leave at two. Listening to more country and not at all missing trees and shade and the sound of scattered gunfire, generals bursting into villages and demanding he kiss a set of stars pinned to a collar. They would have early dinners when he got back, he and Dawn eating sticky rice by the handful, larb, the occasional papaya salad. Laughing in two languages, or, in his case, one and one-third, and watching little David point and ask questions. It was just the three of them then, but it was supposed to be more. They wanted more. Had struggled mightily to get the one, but they prayed every night, in English. Hmong. Whatever languages they could find and without ever losing faith. In succeeding. In actually buying the house. In a future that held a family doctor or lawyer or engineer. They wanted the Dream. They wanted America. They wanted to attend at least two college graduations with real champagne and handshakes from the entire community.

Had they known, they would have settled for one. For David. And they would have been grateful. More than anyone can possibly imagine. They wouldn't have spent so much time looking ahead.

It was one of those summer nights. An American summer night. Humid but rapidly cooling. Neighbors on porches with beer. Charcoal making the air smell burnt and appetizing. They didn't have a grill. But they had money. Not much but enough. His father drove, and they listened to a John Prine cassette on the way to the restaurant. His parents remember very clearly. They sang the words. Dawn's off-key voice more like talking, like a poet, an orator. *Little pictures have big ears. Don't stop to count the years. Sweet songs never last too long on broken radios.* The windows were down. They said "pictures" like "pitures" and "songs" like "sawns." Static crept in through the notes, and David sat between them. He wasn't in a car seat. Just dancing and hopping and shouting about his first hamburger. Mulberry's was the only place, and the drive-thru line snaked all the way out of the lot and way back to Cornhusker Lanes. They didn't care. They kept singing. David kept clapping. Watching people walk in and out with red, white, and blue bags, grease and heat and night air all mixing together. When they finally made it to the front, the voice on the speaker couldn't understand his father. It took three tries. Two hamburgers and a chicken, he said, but what they got from the acned teenager with sweat on his apron was actually a hamburger and two chickens. There was disappointment but no complaint. They just gave David what he wanted and decided to eat in the car. It was his night, after all.

Everything after was a mistake. An accident. A series of mix-ups and oversights that could have happened to anyone. The undercooked food, the hospital thinking it was a routine stomach bug, the doctor yawning and no one quite sure exactly what his father was talking about through the accent and the tears. The whole haze of diagnoses and pacing and bad news delivered as if it were an errand. Three lawyers came to the funeral. Separately. His father kept shaking his head, refusing even to look at them, but one managed to slip a card into Dawn's hand, wrapped inside a handkerchief that looked like the Nebraska state flag. They still have both, tucked in a drawer with court filings, receipts, and a settlement agreement they signed at their own kitchen table, after midnight, coffee mugs empty and too tired to argue about anything else. The card says, "We hold people responsible. It's the American way."

The Messenger

During the Democratic primary, the senatorial candidate made one ironclad promise. If elected, he'd be the best bowler in Congress. Better than Sasse, better than Smith, better than anyone from New York or LA or Wichita. He'd use this skill as a political lubricant, drafting legislation laneside and rolling his way into deals with job-creators and foreign dignitaries.

At first, his whole staff thought this was an oddball joke or maybe a too-clever bit of electoral strategy (and they warned him about Mondale falling on his ass, to which he replied, "That comparison is a personal insult"), but then he went ahead and made the idea the centerpiece of his whole campaign. Rather than visit every county, he visited every listed bowling alley. All 114. Called each stop a "Rally at the Alley" and appended Roman numerals to each one like they were Super Bowls. In fact, some of the places were called Super Bowls. Super Bowl Grand Island (Rally at the Alley XCV), Super Bowl Alliance (III), Super Bowl Chadron (I). There was Husker Lanes in Ogallala (VII) and Starz & Strikes in Plattsmouth (CXIV). At every stop, he bowled three games (usually in jeans and a John Cougar Mellencamp T-shirt), each with (zero in the beginning, then one, and then, by popular demand) three different, randomly chosen registered voters, and after each frame he got on the PA and answered a question, supposedly from the crowd and drawn out of the biggest bowling shoe his top aide could find. Most of the time, the questions weren't even about politics, and, by the end of tour, everyone knew his favorite ice cream (graham cracker), the name of his dog (Truman), and where he was on January 2, 1996 (at a bar in Kearney with two Native guys (one the best bowler he'd ever met) and his (then future) wife Elaine watching "the greatest run ever made by a college football player, or, no, wait, anybody who ever played football, whether it be American or European or Australian").

In Scottsbluff (V, where he bowled a 760 series), it was noon, and the only people there were two men drinking High Life and maybe a dozen Hispanics celebrating the birthday of a girl who looked about eight. By the final third of Lincoln (CI, CII, 599 ("nerves") and 826 (!), respectively), they'd switched to exclusively evening rallies (and had enough money to buy French fries and chicken wings and pizza) and were competing with fire code to the point that people had to be turned away. It got so intense that there was the natural backlash from his primary opponents (and even the Republican incumbent, though everyone admitted (when pressed) that he had beautiful form, the way he slid and kicked the right foot out and left it hanging slightly off the ground like an open gate), most of which centered around the fact that the candidate never seemed to talk about anything remotely resembling policy. There were competing theories as to why this was. The presumptive front-runner at the outset (a woman from Lincoln, trained as a lawyer and with an ambitious agenda regarding health care and common-sense firearm restrictions and "farm-friendly," environmental regs) floated a rigged-shoe theory suggesting that all substantive questions disappeared sometime between deposit and proclamation. Meanwhile, the incumbent claimed (none too subtly) that the attendees must have been too stupid, too stoned, and/or too over-sexed to ask anything resembling a real question. At one of the debates, the candidate was asked about all of this, and he said, "Listen, way Washington is now, no junior senator's gonna be able to do anything landmark, and even if by some Frank Capra miracle he does, he ain't gonna have control over the specifics, so you might as well vote for someone you like. Might as well vote for someone who's on your team." And, to some (relatively mild) surprise, people did. It looked dicey until certain areas of Lincoln and Omaha started coming in, but, once they reported, he won by 4 points.

At the victory party (Chop's in Omaha (CV and CXV, 747 and 701)), they went cosmic. A reporter asked if he was finally going to talk turkey during the general, and he said, "Who needs to talk about it when you can do it, and I got three of 'em already tonight." The crowd roared, his staff struck up "Authority Song," and the (campaign-proclaimed) "greatest Husker since William Jennings Bryan" bowled another wobbly (some would say lucky) strike.

Old-Fashioned Rustlers

Back in high school, Adler knew this girl named Delaney. Her cousins kept horses in these stables out near Gothenburg, and she used to sneak us in late at night. We'd sit around on hay bales drinking Grain Belts. Sometimes I'd head outside and smoke so they could do their thing, and sometimes we'd just lay there watching the animals sleep and talking about how she wanted to go to vet school and Adler and I were pretty much destined to die right around here.

One night, we split a whole case, and she stripped down to a sports bra and them spandex pants and told us it was time to saddle up. We rode in the dark. Alongside the interstate. Delaney charged onto the shoulder, and we watched semis screaming by and laying on their horns, and we didn't know if it was out of anger or fear or else just straight up lust.

After a while, we found the railroad tracks. There was a line of abandoned boxcars, and we tied up the horses and pretended the graffiti didn't exist. We ate apples. Left the cores to rot on cold metal. Delaney pulled out three longnecks, and we drank them in four big pulls, and, when they were empty, we stood them on the rails mouth ends down. I said I felt like a hobo. The sun was coming up behind the Ag West and across the tracks. Adler sighed and threw his bottle toward the highway, and as the glass shattered, he looked at Delaney and me and said he'd give anything for it to be 1866.

Fish Stories

Then there was the summer we rented out three cabins at the Trade Winds and Pike brought his new girlfriend. She was 28. Worked as a nurse in Grand Island and looked like one of them actresses might show up in a commercial. The boys kept running around and tossing the football at her feet so they could get a look down her shirt, but nobody cared enough to stop them, not even her. We were happy they had something to do. We let them steal a couple beers. Watched them dive headfirst into the reservoir. We sat by a fire drinking cases of Busch and sent Pike over to Loup City to pick up a pizza from the bowling alley while the girl told us a few stories about how he was a real Christian these days, and we laughed when he came back two hours later, drunker than when he left.

"Jesus drank wine," she said, and we agreed, though not this much of it. And probably didn't drive home neither. She said that was because He didn't have a car, and we said He could have conjured one up if He wanted, and then there was an argument about riding camels and whether any man in our state could stay on top of the humps.

Pike just kept staring at the fire. He took off his shoes. Threw the pizza box in. He let out some kind of yell, and we thought we could make out "Geronimo," but mostly what I remember is seeing his foot on the cardboard and flames around his kneecaps and then old Pike howling in the water, the boys looking at him in fear, or maybe something closer to awe.

The next day, the leg was red and puffy and blistered, but Pike was still up at 5:00 AM and backing the boat down the ramp. We let the boys sleep. Left the girl at the cabin and told her she could give them toast for breakfast. That or else all she had to do was prance around in his double-X Springsteen T-shirt, and they'd be good and entertained. She laughed. Pike winked at her. Then, he went out and caught more walleye than we'd ever seen. Sometimes they'd flop out of the cooler and onto the deck, and, pole in one hand, beer in another, he'd just scoop them up and flip them right back in. I said he looked like a fat-ass Tommie Frazier, but you went even further. You said, "The way he's reeling them fuckers in, I'm thinking this ain't the Sherman Reservoir. I'm thinking we're in the presence of greatness, and this here's the Sea of Galilee."

Message to the Grassroots

The consultants assessed the restaurant's overall position as surprisingly strong. Yes, it was a crisis, but it was not insurmountable. For starters, there was just the one incident, and, though it was tragic and involved a consumer of unfortunate age, the two of them had seen much worse. They also complimented the overall food safety protocols and training guidelines, calling them "abundantly clear regarding internal temperature and fully in accordance with FDA requirements" and arguing that this made the response both relatively straightforward and almost certain to succeed.

Their recommendations were as follows: "Find an attractive employee. It should be a woman, and she should be pretty in a motherly way, by which we mean in possession of a visual appeal that isn't overtly sexual. Mid-30s to early-40s. Has an ability to speak with or affect compassion and is comfortable in front of cameras. Capable of memorizing paragraphs of moderate length and then delivering them with fluidity. If you cannot find her among the current ranks, we can supply a desirable stand-in, though in the case of questions (interactive press conferences are preferable, as they convey a sense of openness and courage) an internal option (who may have to be promised promotion, though it should be backdated or delayed so as not to appear either reactionary or *quid pro quo*) is best as it is more likely to produce an authentic response. She should express sympathy but not regret. Invoke the word 'tragedy' but frame events as unavoidable. The product of a single, former employee who has been terminated but whose plight and general state of mind she finds must be painful to even imagine. Call it a 'regrettable lapse of concentration by a former employee working a part-time job, a former employee who is, of course, ultimately responsible but under circumstances that could have befallen any one of us.' At some point, it may become necessary to produce said (former) employee for public consumption. For apology and potentially cathartic excoriation. If he's reluctant, compensation may have to be authorized. In the event that he's angry, bitter, psychologically unstable, or otherwise unappealing, a substitute can (again) be arranged, though it will involve two financial disbursements (as well as the express, affirmative permission of the original (former) employee) instead of one. We do recommend any potential substitute be white and male, ideally with blue eyes and a generally "American" appearance. Acting experience a plus, New York scene preferred in order to minimize the possibility of present and/or future recognition. Should it become necessary, it is our view that implementing this part of the recommended strategy will require the most caution, fraught as it is with the potential for loose ends and subsequent media backlash. For example, imagine an enterprising reporter from the *World-Herald*. He senses something off about your response or is perhaps simply engaging in conspiratorial wishful thinking. He goes to Ogallala and starts asking questions. At the diner on Main St., he hears a Vietnam vet talking about the 'kid that cooked the deadly hamburger' and finds some 19-year-old named Arnie who lives with his parents and has become too depressed to get out of bed. The kitchen is freshly remodeled, and there's a brand-new Ford Mustang in the garage, except the kid doesn't drive it anymore because it's January by now, and everything's covered in a thin layer of ice and the thing has rear-wheel drive. Not to mention, every time he climbed inside he thought about that kid and his family and blasted the radio and gassed up to 105 and considered swerving into the South Platte. Stay with us now. The parents are dying to talk, and they let loose with everything. The orchestration, the pay-off, the swap we managed to pull off, and five months from now you're looking at a second crisis, and this time the threat will be existential. In our experience, they'll swallow the act. It's the perceived lie they won't live with, and care must be taken. If he's any good, the reporter will ask them about taking the money, and maybe you'll be able to hammer them there, or maybe they just offer to give it back. There's no downside for them. The offer itself is sufficient for their credibility, and if you do indeed take it then you're only admitting the whole charade and accepting everything that goes with such an admission, which is, basically, see 'existential threat' above. Meaning ironclad NDAs will be necessary. Protection against personal lawsuits directed at this (former) employee (who will, to reiterate, be the subtle locus of blame in such a way as to (in all likelihood) provide ample legal ammunition) and filed on behalf of the bereaved. Dispatching friendly attorneys to the victim's family, attorneys inclined to preach the Gospel of Settlement, has worked wonders in previous cases. It's a path we endorse. Pay for dead ends now rather than becoming roadkill later. In public, this employee will be a sympathetic scapegoat, but in private he will be under your protection, and we urge you to save your frugality for something else. An ad campaign, perhaps, which will be the next logical step. Our research suggests something low-fi. Something emphasizing individual responsibility. The unavoidability of danger and its corresponding allure. Strange as it sounds, you should play up the crisis, and we recommend a series of commercials featuring a lone hero. He is an archetype, a cowboy, and he goes into your restaurant over the objections of his friends. 'It's too dangerous' they say, but he (or, better yet, she) is impervious, rugged and confident. We've tested various taglines, and the one that really moves dials is 'Try to Control Yourself.' Our assessment is they won't be able to. Our assessment is you'll come out even stronger. Indeed, there is opportunity in tragedy, and you should never fail to capitalize on a chance to rebrand."

Till Death

They were throwing a football back and forth in the cemetery behind the church. The groom said he didn't want to go through with it. The best man stuck his chin out and then looked at the bride's brothers, who were over by the cooler grabbing a couple of beers. Both of them had removed their sport coats. Their sleeves were rolled up, and you could see the sweat stains from a mile away.

"Tell you what let's do," said the groom, and he patted the ball with his left hand. "You run a thirty-yard post, and I'll put this thing right on Uncle Georgie's grave. Catch it, and we'll go back inside. If not, you can sneak my ass out while they're doing Delilah's hair."

The best man took off on instinct. The groom started a five-step drop. The bride's brothers watched a high, tight spiral with dumb smiles on their faces, and one of them said, "At least the son of a bitch can throw." As the ball came down, the best man imagined it was a baby. Or a missile. He considered the sun and the Earth's rate of rotation and knew he'd never concentrated this hard in his entire life. He dove toward the headstone. Curled his fingers around the ball. His back smashed against granite, and he thought about bruises and loyalty and whether he should drop it on purpose, or if maybe there were some things a man needed to learn on his own.

Warriors

Because I used to be pretty good at football, they like to send me these invites to speak at high schools around the state. I say no a lot, but sometimes things line up or I need the money, and inevitably there'll be a Q and A, and some kid will ask what I remember most. He'll think I'm gonna talk about the Big XII Championship or the Fiesta Bowl, and so by the time I finish it's mostly just prairie silence. Crickets and aphids whispering at night.

I tell them about the kid from Sidney coming across the middle. How I blew him up good, and he made a sound like an empty milk jug. I say, the way he was lying there, the high-fives, the grass in my facemask, that's all flickering. It goes in and out, and sometimes the details change. His angle on the ground or where the ball is or how long we kneel in prayer. What I really remember is how, the next Monday at practice, we still didn't know if he was gonna walk again, and Coach Bradley brought us together first thing. He called us men. He told us to listen up. He said I did everything right and that was just football, and we are defined by our response to things beyond our control. My teammates kept pounding my shoulder pads softly. I thought about God and my parents and this girl Leigh I used to watch from the sidelines on Friday nights. Then Coach said he wanted a sharp practice. Hit with your heads up, but don't let it keep you from hitting hard. He said he wanted a "Warriors" on three, and we came together and shouted like we meant it. Like we believed every single word.

Dissent

If you start at the Golden Spike Tower and then travel a couple miles straight southeast, won't be long before you come to a clapboard neighborhood along Buffalo Bill Avenue hung up between living and struggling and full-on dead and buried. There's a house up there, two stories plus and higher than anything else on the block, siding kind of a forest green ripened to inner lime. Used to be owned by a man townsfolk liked to call "Hollow," though his Christian certificate said Apex Hollinfell. He wasn't exactly atypical, least not compared to the frontier types we've been seeing for a hundred years, but there was always something I guess you could call defiant in him. Something stubborn and aggressive, beyond even the pioneer norm. Used to ride through quiet neighborhoods in a pickup at 4:00 AM, for example. Honking the horn and blaring Whalen or maybe John Prine and yelling, "It's another dark morning in America, folks, and damned if y'all ain't missing every last sign." Storm out of the Old Scout downtown after some kind a rant about getting back to the gold standard, lighting bills on fire and saying how it wasn't nothing but paper. That sort of thing. We might a been able to ignore most of it. All that brash talk and flashy frustration. But it was something quieter. More opaque. Something he did on his own property, on his own time, that no one's gonna soon forget.

Every afternoon, after hauling lumber to every farm needing it between here and Ogallala, Hollow would grab a half-rusted Werner, make his way up to his roof with a six-pack of High Life, cans bonded together with fish-death plastic, and drink while staring out at the old rail station off to the west. Was up there from around

5:00 until 7:00 or so, draining beers one by one and then tossing each can down onto his lawn, hoping, everyone said, they'd form some prophetic pattern, like Tarot or tea leaves or some other of those Oriental arts. Folks that got close enough thought they could hear him mumbling too. Spouting haikus, maybe. Repeating lines from William Jennings Bryan. Jimbo Larsen says it was "nothin' but curses and quotes from old episodes of *The Twilight Zone*, only with the tone pitched like just so. Almost sounding even enough to make you wonder if it was you that was missing something. Like you was the weird one for just shaking your head and shuffling away ashamed instead of leaning in to listen."

Worst of it was, when there were six beers empty and scattered on the lawn, he'd climb down from the roof and stand out on grass or leaves or snow or maybe under stars, all depending, of course, on certain details of positioning to do with the status of Earth's rotating revolution. Then he'd stare and spit and pop in a plug of Copenhagen and start to gather all those cans back up, always just one at a time, holding each by the built-in opener and scanning for dents before moving onto the next, eventually juggling all six and opening the door with his elbows on the way back inside. He looked like some kind of crime scene investigator out there, all planned and careful and divining some future he could see just a bit further into. Like, in spite of all the bluster and chaos, maybe our Jimbo was right. Maybe there really was something only Hollow could figure.

It went on for years and in all kinds of weather. Raindrops thick as gravy, ice clinging to shingles, 95-degree steam drifting in visible distortion off the black, even were reports of him sitting up there during a certified twister, touched down just across the South Platte. Neighbors could only shake their heads, smile even. It was what they gossiped about down at the Old Scout, preferring to do their own drinking indoors, talking in these guffawed whispers you give when you start questioning your own vision. "Railroad used to stop here," they said. "Was the end of the goddamn world for all anyone knew. Which means you're just bound to attract folks like that. Whole generations of 'em, even. Melvin Lundstrum driving his car into the river on a dare and his pop walking around town with that smile like he's proud. Willa Frederick sleeping in the cemetery every Friday night like there's something she can do to bring old Maverick back. Just folks looking for some small thing to control, some personal ritual to give 'em any little patch a meaning. Times what they are, place what it is, you're always gonna get a few like Apex. People without no real sense. People don't realize we went and turned into this big empty middle. Ain't no edge to this place no more, and he's just the latest one trying to make his own." They'd go at his mind like the feds probe killers, farmers and landscapers and small-town teachers all trying a hand at diagnosis, even if some form a "Prairie Madness" was all anyone could ever chalk it up to in the end.

The last day he was up there was July. Has to be two years ago now. Right in the middle of the drought that almost bankrupted the Wilkens' place and caused the whole town to show up to that meeting with Senator Grossbuckle, worrying about subsidy reform and water shortages, folks acting polite but cussing Lincoln and Omaha under their breath. Enough going on that you could've been forgiven for forgetting, just for a moment, about ol' Hollow, even if this is the kind of place where no one did.

Started simple enough from what I hear. Hollow up there on his roof and about to finish can number two, number one having landed mouth end down almost near the exact corner of his driveway and communal sidewalk. He must have been about to toss that second one when he saw Laney Broadplain, wearing a floral print sun dress and carrying her hands on her hips "like always," she says. She swears she was only trying to be neighborly. Have one of those honest civic conversations used to be the fabric of democracy and all that. Express herself without getting too personal, if that's even possible with "a kook like him."

"Hollow," she said, she claims with a smile, "You got a minute to chat?"

"You can make yourself heard ain't like I can run away," which Laney says she knew was as close as she was ever gonna get to an invitation.

"Alright then," she began, "Not sure there's no smooth way to bring it up, but me and Big Bill are fixing to sell our place down the block." She pointed, with her thumb, back over her shoulder. "We got the open house tomorrow and folks might be comin' by on their own time from now till we get a good offer."

Hollow didn't toss so much as drop a can then. Managed to land about four feet from her. Wasn't threatening, she didn't think, just that he couldn't start in on another while the previous one was anywhere near the same vertical location. "Good luck to ya," he said, nodding and holding his ear right up to that next can as he levered it open.

"We was wondering if you might take it easy for a bit you don't mind my asking. Just two weeks or so. Long enough we got a fair chance at full price. We'd be real obliged." She saw him take a sip that appeared meant to facilitate some kind of inner calm, though, in practice. Well.

"How you gonna talk down with me way up here?" he said.

"What? I's just—"

"I'm supposed to be aidin' and abettin' you trying to drive up some price?"

"Asking for a small, neighborly favor is all."

"Seems like you trying to get some dig in. Like me sittin' up here on my own bought and paid for property's gonna submarine some 'investment' you and Bill hoping to cash in on, even though you been sleepin' under that roof for fifteen years now. House don't owe you nothin'."

Laney stopped looking at him then, instead staring down at her shoes, so she didn't notice he'd gone into kind of a squat, waiting for the chance to go full-on erect. "Ain't trying to hurt no feelings. All I wanted—"

"You're gonna have to speak up. Can't hear mumblin' too good."

She did look up then and watched him swirl the can in circles, hearing a faint kind of liquid splash like there couldn't be much left. "You ever gonna sell this place, Hollow?"

"Ain't planning on it."

"Well. If you do. Or even if you can just imagine. Not like we're being dishonest here. All we're hoping is to fetch a decent price. Market value, like they say. On account of we put a lot of effort into that place, and it'd be nice to see some of it pay off like in a material sense."

Hollow spit from up there. Got it within about two feet of her. "Real estate," he said. "Shit, they never stop gaming you, do they? Everybody buying what they can't afford and then turning around and charging some fish more than he can afford and everyone all optimistic about some profit on down the line that's just as imaginary as that southern border. Hate to tell ya, sweetheart, but ain't nothin' there."

She watched him stand up and launch a can came down just behind her. He took two steps forward, and there was the sound a rubber sole makes on cheap metal, an equally cheap echo dripping from the rain spout down to where she was standing, wondering if he was fixing to let himself fall. Like some kind of test, she said, as if her status as his neighbor would depend on how willing she was to catch him. Or even get in his way.

"North Platte," he shouted, pointing, "You been good and dead since they built I-80, and you might as well embrace it. 'Cause you think some bit of marketing's gonna save you, well, then you'll just have to endure dyin' all over again. And so sayeth ol' Hollow Apex and so forth." After which he sat back down slowly, opening another beer and staring out toward the west, eyes glazed in this icy and dismissive way like he was done with her. Having no patience for anything else.

"I swear," she said later, "Never seen no look that crazy. Otherworldly almost. Like I's just some old busybody out to hassle the neighbors. I mean, we had our share, but wasn't never me, and you think he'd know that much at least. And, anyway, I maybe shoulda stayed out there. Shoulda seen it comin', you know? Even if we never thought he's anyone to take too serious. I keep fearin' alls I did was make somethin' already hard even harder, and ain't no excuse for that."

No excuse for insanity, either, townsfolk kept telling her. Even from right after. Medics staring wide-eyed at a crumpled heap and half the town's force out in his front yard, lights bluing up the early evening, neighbors in gym shorts and robes, a couple folks sitting on a porch with coffee or scotch, saying they heard the crash about 45 minutes after some shouting and then saw him lying there, face down and twisted at an odd angle right near the sidewalk, one beer can they found half-empty still up on the roof. Cops looked through the whole scene like he used to for a while, asked Laney a few questions, and then sort of shrugged in that tragic way, like what can anyone do to stop someone ain't all there in the first place, though for a time she felt like somehow he fell on her shoulders, like had to be something she said or did or failed to intimate with all the subtleties, the verbal and nonverbal ticks, drawn up around tactful Midwestern speech. Was a moment there everyone thought she might turn crazy herself, just from the unknown of it, but she's doing better now, thankfully. On account of some old partner in the lumber delivery business told her Hollow never would've taken no civic confrontation seriously, not to mention that wasn't no way he'd a left half a beer unfinished if he was planning anything sinister. Nah, she could do all the blaming she wanted, but accidents will happen and some folks always stride that line between falling and flying and so on and she should just save that grief and keep her head up for the next thing coming down the line.

Tell you what, though, and this is just one opinion so no need to run off looking for next of kin or hollering about some kind of conspiracy. And it's nothing to do with Laney, but you do start to wonder if ol' Hollow might deserve just a little more consideration. Even a little credit. Because two stories and change really ain't all that high. And for what happened to happen, well, you need more than just blind luck, whatever kind it is. You need maybe just a bit of intention. Some kind of familiarity with angles and rotations. All those evenings up there, staring out into the sunset, looking at this great barren center we all come to be surrounded by. Start to wonder if maybe he wasn't performing calculations. If he wasn't some kind of amateur physicist. And death ain't something that can only be talked about scientifically, with trajectories and vectors and measurements of impact, but you can't commit to that kind of routine without picking up certain patterns. Making certain inferences regarding the various forces that happen to be what the old timers would call aswirl. Ain't just gravity. Meters per second squared and all that classroom babble. It's something else too, and Hollow maybe really could see it clearer. Hear some antenna scrabbled voices from above as much as below. Saying alls it takes is a little focus. Saying study hard as you can, and maybe you'll just happen to learn.

2nd

Quarter

Roadside America

Around about a year ago, I'm coming back from a job in Stapleton. Headed into town on 83, and this had to be November. Sometime between Cidnee cutting bait and the rest of us getting Marietta to commit to Heartland. It's one of them nights you're surprised how dark it is at five o'clock. Windy too. Truck's veering a little toward the center line, and I'm trying not to overcorrect but I do and thank God for the rumble strip because there's a woman out there by herself on the shoulder with a camera hanging from her neck. And I mean a real camera. Got a flash bulb and everything. So I get safely by her, and I pull over. I'm thinking, what in the hell is she doing, the fucking nut. Could have been killed. Could get lost or snatched up by one of them long-hauls always coming through, and doesn't she watch the news? Maybe she's one of them artist types just don't know where she's at half the time, but Christ almighty, the sheer fucking ignorance. Somebody's got to enlighten her, and I take it upon myself. Start heading back to where she's standing waving my arms a little so she knows I'm a man means no harm. "Ma'am," I say, but she just keeps on standing there, back to me, snapping away at some asphalt or gravel or prairie grass or what have you. But then I get a little closer, and I can see the side of her face, and this is important, alright? Is that she ain't pretty. Got short hair and one of them rat noses, and she ain't particularly ugly neither, but there's not much for me there if you understand, so let's get that out of the way. But I see what she's taking pictures of, and it's a dead raccoon. Big fucker. Teeth hanging out belly up. Must be pretty fresh because it ain't smell yet and I don't see no hawks circling. Little pools of blood barely dry too. I gotta be ten feet from her by now, and I don't want to scare the poor thing, so I stop.

"You alright there, Missy?" I say, loud enough she has to hear, and she just puts her hand up. So, I wait. She turns to face one of them gray sunsets and takes two more photos. Then, without even looking at me, she says, "Do you know how many animal carcasses there are on Nebraska highways at any given moment?"

Now, I don't have to tell you that I don't have the first, which is exactly what I tell her.

"Got to be hundreds," she says, "Maybe thousands."

"All in places no one should get stuck alone I imagine," hoping she'll get the hint.

"What I want to do is photograph all of them. Every last one. Get as many as I can. Deer. Raccoons. Opossums. Squirrels, rabbits, skunks. Bears if there's a car big enough. Or sandhill cranes or bobcats or coyotes or whatever else we got. Line them all up in this exact kind of light right here. Put them in nice even frames. Nice rows like tic-tac-toe with little pools of blood dripping toward the borders. I want to send the whole thing to *National Geographic* and just call it 'America.' Something easy and simple like that. Or else 'Nebraska,' and, hell, maybe I do one for each state, like they got with those quarters, and then people can collect the whole gorgeous set."

Now, this whole time she ain't even looking at me. Just snapping away. Swear she was still going on about maybe buying out billboards or setting up a little roadside museum and so caught up she didn't even hear me going back to the truck. And so as I drive away I'm looking at her in the rearview and watching her get smaller and knowing, Christ, the next time I run into something at 2:00 AM her face is gonna be the first thing on my mind, and couldn't it've at least looked like Jolene from the Old Scout back when she was 24? And it makes me an asshole, I know, but that's what I was thinking, and the shame of it is I ain't hit nothing since, and I still can't stop thinking about her. Been driving around so much I got roadkill in my goddamn dreams. Just last week, you know Jimbo Larsen lives out Homestead Road? He tells me he ran into a whitetail the night before on I-80 and what do I do but ask him where exactly and practically beg for the mile number so I can go out and have a look. I don't know if maybe I think she might be there or if it's some kind of same-place, different-time thrill I'm after, but I do. I go. Early morning had to be 5:00, 6:00 AM, and I find the spot alright, but the deer's gone. Don't know if the county came and got it or maybe some scavenger, but alls I see is a few red stains. Big semis racing by and honking, and I'm on my knees feeling the pavement, and the whole thing must look ridiculous. It's cold, and I'm gulping coffee from a thermos too. Looking out at this field's got a layer of frost on it. A few trees in the distance. It's beautiful and brown and empty, and I must have hit the coffee too fast because I start to feel sick. My head is pounding, and I swear, I almost fucking hurled. But I didn't. I watched wind running across the prairie, and I somehow held it together. I somehow managed to keep it all in.

Supply and Demand

The gun that killed Marietta's cousin was supposed to end up in Saudi Arabia (as part of a deal the President said would "solidify our strategic security alliance with a vital regional ally"), but instead it was sent to Jordan and later included in a shipment to a Kurdish militia group in Syria, which group then lost it or sold it or gave it to an ill-fated unit that was overrun on the outskirts of Raqqa and stripped of all artillery. Nobody would explain the conflicting destinations (perhaps because nobody, least of all Marietta, knew enough to ask), but maybe that was for the best since no answer could undo the death of a 20-year-old Bears fan from Custer County, and, anyway, it was all very complicated.

About the only thing that could be said for certain was that the weapon was made from aluminum smelted by Alcoa at a processing facility in Bettendorf, IA, and then sold to the Department of Defense as part of a $50 million military supply contract negotiated by Wilton Barrera, a Pittsburgh-born, Georgetown-educated lawyer with an office on K Street. Barrera was known primarily for being a Pirates diehard (who would sit through multiple, hours-long rain delays on dreary April days at PNC just to see the final three outs of a 7-3 loss to the Padres or Diamondbacks) and (in certain circles) for having a weakness for the $400 handjobs provided by an upscale "spa" in Bethesda, a service he was once covertly filmed enjoying next to a sitting senator from Delaware. Luckily for Wilton, the senator garnered much more media interest. He claimed he'd only recently begun working with "Mr. Barrera," and neither of them knew what they were in for, and, by the time he figured it out, it was halfway too late. If you watched the video closely, he said, if you went frame-by-frame, you could see him confused, resisting, trying to push away the young woman's (whose name he was pretty sure was Cheyenne, and of course no one had bothered to film the pleasant, rather heartfelt conversation they'd been having about her two jobs and mountain of student debt and sheer terror at the prospect of losing her health care subsidy) hand, unsure of what was actually happening and not even really enjoying it. Of course, this wasn't enough to prevent a forced resignation, and he was out of work for a while, a year maybe, long enough for the news cycle to turn over a few thousand times, but then he started a lobbying firm and managed to attract an array of industrial clients, including Alcoa and U.S. Ordnance, the latter of which had him out to Reno at least three times a year for strategy sessions and (more often than not) celebration. At some point during each trip, the VPs du jour would start expensing drinks, and they'd all end up near a strip club or brothel outside of town (up in the desert practically), kill the engines of their cars, and sit there debating whether or not they should go in. Sometimes they would, and sometimes they'd just down six-packs of Budweiser and see who could toss the empties farthest out into the night. But, each and every time, the senator would look around and say, "I don't know how much you know about me, but I got to admit, most days I look at myself in the mirror, and I say, 'Goddamn it, Senator, why haven't you been working with these assholes your whole life?'" Then, he'd always propose a toast to "making up for lost time," and they'd all laugh, and eventually someone would drive him back to his hotel, where he'd flop face-down on the bed and dream about football, about state championships and cheerleaders and free donuts at the local diner, all while feeling seasick and thrilled and expectant about next time, about a life well-lived and another job just really damn well done.

Spirit Guide

Alejandra's father was in Nebraska by himself for a while. She must have been four and five years old. He lived in a trailer between Grand Island and Kearney and spent his days butchering dead cows. He did it so much he couldn't shake hands at the end. His fingers were permanently curled.

When she got to high school, they rented a house near the highway, and she found a box of letters he'd sent back home. They mentioned canned food and space heaters and hiding next to the Windex during raids. She asked him about that part of his life, and, because she always wanted to know everything for certain and for sure and forever, she recorded his response on a cassette tape she keeps in a drawer by her bed. The thread is unspooling a little now, but if you find the right recorder or an old enough car you can still hear her wondering how he managed. How he survived and kept them together for as long as he did.

His answer is choppy. It sounds half-serious. You have to filter out the static and be careful with the translation. What he says is most of the raids were orchestrated. Political. They got advanced notice, and the diving into cupboards was nothing more than a game of hide-and-seek. For the others, he developed a strategy. It was one he'd recommend to this day. You find yourself an Indian, he says. Mine was named John, but they called him Running Tree, and we met in a bar off a Route 30. He taught me to bowl and play darts and curse in Lakota, and that was essential for blending in because they see you with Mexicans, they think Mexican, and then la migra gets called. But they see you with Indians, they think

Indian, and then what they do is laugh. They buy you a drink. And most of them don't even bother to see you at all.

The Computer Wore Tennis Shoes

Location services are on, and they're saying she's at 42.1423° N, 102.8580° W and looking at something called Carhenge. Search identifies it as a re-creation of the famous Salisbury Plain tableaux (featuring the husks of old cars (hence the name)) just west of the Nebraska Sandhills. Calendar wants to know why she isn't back at the hotel in Sidney, prepping for the client meeting she has in 45 minutes (and wonders whether she even attended her 1:00 PM with the distributor), while Maps (which wasn't asked for directions but turned on automatically when she got within five miles of a patch of land assigned to the United States Air Force and housing an LGM-30 Minuteman III intercontinental ballistic missile) says her current position is almost 90 miles away, and there's not a chance in hell she can make it. This is when Mail chimes in and says it's catalogued a series of notes from her boss that its tone algo reads as frantic, and Messaging recites a text from her husband demonstrating at least mild concern (which further worries Accounts because it's got a transaction record confirming the purchase of a fifth of Karkov ("a product not exactly made for refined enjoyment," according to Reviews) at a dive grocer off 385 and the knowledge that her alcohol consumption is limited almost exclusively to bottles of Prosecco and Chardonnay she gets on discount at the Northern Lights Hy-Vee in Lincoln). Photo isn't paying attention to any of it. It's just snapping pictures of stacked gray Cadillacs framed by a slowly falling Panhandle sun. Social has a theory she's meeting an ex-boyfriend (based on a recent reconnection and several DMs regarding "that night in my cousin's barn when we sat on hay bales and listened to owls and cats and drank Grain Belts until it felt like we were on fine linen"), but News posits an anxiety attack brought on by a sudden interest in politics, global terrorism, and North Korea (though Mail argues it isn't sudden at all and directs their attention to a message sent two years ago to a friend in D.C., the text of which is just begging for comfort and dripping with the kind of fear Search can only find in archived historical correspondence (as in letters from soldiers and certain high-level communications from October 1962) and, furthermore, highlights a (recently deleted) draft of an email that discusses a growing spiritual hunger, an itch, it says, a pure fucking need to find what she called "the heart of America" (a place Maps informs them is technically located (assuming she means the contiguous center) 363.5 miles away in Lebanon, KS (where an NGS marker, an American flag, and a small chapel identify the exact location for tourists and passersby))). This inspires collective concern, so they manage (through Gallery) to gain access to every image Photo's ever taken and (based on the two most recent albums (the contents of which include shots of her (at her 10-year reunion) standing next to her first-year college roommate (who grew up in Omaha but now mostly sticks close to her Colorado monastery) near a lake on the campus of a Benedictine college in Minnesota and a picture of the only other person at Carhenge this afternoon (a woman who looks 50 and has a neck tattoo and no wedding ring and appears to be waving or nodding in greeting/approval))) deduce two things. One, she's clearly at a crossroads and hoping to be moved in one direction or the other by the sheer automotive mysticism of her surroundings, and two, she's jealous and regretful and looking around thinking something along the lines of, "Maybe these two have the right idea."

From here, they reason that she'll eventually go back to whatever's left of her life, and, when she does, Revenue will show her an ad for a divorce lawyer based near the university. Of course, they can't be certain. But their best guess is she'll (probably) decide to give him a call.

Dog Day Afternoon

We named the dog Kinsey because he humped everything in sight. Legs, chairs, shoes, you name it. He was this German shepherd we got from the shelter, and we laughed about it at first, but then he went after the kid from down the block. Accidentally bit the little guy right near the neck, and it barely drew blood, but of course the parents complained to the neighborhood association, and they held a meeting with lots of shouting and talk of lawsuits, and, in the end, we promised to put him down.

I remember the day we did it. We bought him a Heart Attack Platter at the Mulberry's off the interstate and let him eat out of the bag in the waiting room. At some point, you put a blindfold on him and stuck an unlit cigarette in his mouth, and people looked at us like we were assholes. They held their leashes tight because the other dogs were going mad with yipping and claws scratching on tile, and an old lady said, "You think this is a joke, don't you?" but you told her we just wanted to make it all a little more humane. When they called us in, he still had half an order of fries left. We made eye contact. I almost shoved Kinsey into the backseat and drove us 800 miles away.

Dear Abbey

I remember when you told me you weren't a virgin. It was in your brother's truck the summer before your senior year. You were going back to Lincoln, and I was doing landscaping and thinking about classes at MCC. We were drunk. The river was high, and we kept talking about what kind of year the Huskers would have. We started kissing, and then I tried to go up your shirt, but you were wearing one of those tank tops with the built-in bra and so I never made it. You pulled away. "I've done it before, you know," you said, and I nodded and moved back in. That's when you told me you had to be better. That you were going into the novitiate after graduation, probably somewhere in Colorado, and you wanted to look out your window and see mountains. I asked if you'd move to North Dakota with me because I heard there were all kinds of jobs in the oil fields, but you just laughed. You said, "You'll kill yourself, you idiot," and punched me in the shoulder. Your hand felt good. I wanted you to do it again.

I did live in North Dakota for a while. I rented a room in a trailer with two other guys. It always smelled like sweat and Hamburger Helper. My roommates were named Mike and Rick, and sometimes we'd pick up girls at these bars in the middle of nowhere. You can play blackjack in some of them, which I think is better than keno. Anyway, we each bought a stereo so we could have a little more privacy if things went right. Either that or Mike would say, "Anyone feel like a cigarette?" and Rick and I would go outside with our girls if we had any. We would smoke and look at the stars, and it's real pretty out there. Flatter than Nebraska even and quiet like you never heard. I used to think I could see all the way to California, but Rick said it would be Washington or Oregon, only he couldn't remember which.

I miss it sometimes. I moved back when Dad got sick, and we just watched the game together. Mom told us to drink as many Coors as we wanted and bought two cases. We built a pyramid out of the empties, and the Rockies keep looking out at me and asking if you're asleep or on your knees in prayer. I heard the nuns don't let you get letters from men, and there's a note on the website about no email either, and so I'm sorry if this gets you in trouble. Lately I been feeling like I have a way of doing that, and I don't know if they'll see my name and burn it or maybe make you do a Rosary for penance, but you were always the smart one, and I guess I just miss the way you could always tell me what to do.

Penance

The Priest was there every day between one and four. No one ever saw him anywhere else. Never heard him say Mass or sat near him at Hank's Café. But there he was. Every day.

He'd look at them all as they walked in, lawyers, judges, defendants, family. Ask if they needed confession. If he could absolve them. The judges scoffed. The lawyers laughed. Most of the family cried, and the defendants said, "I'm innocent, Father." I never knew what to do.

Every day, he dressed the same. His bald head was perpetually uncovered and his Roman collar always neatly starched. When it snowed, flakes would gather on his skull and cheeks, looking angelically white against his reddened skin. Every now and then, someone would accept his offer, and the two of them would walk to the bottom of the steps and confer quietly, whispering. The Priest would lay his hands on the penitent's forehead and mumble things in Latin, and then the two would part ways. Occasionally, the county prosecutor could be seen prowling around these meetings, leaning in, trying to look nonchalant. His name was Jan, and he was tall and blond and smelled like dust and vinegar.

He once asked me to transcribe them for him, the confessions. I thought he was kidding. But maybe it would have helped.

Most of the litigation that came through our county was small time. Lots of speeding tickets. Shoplifters. The occasional college student caught with marijuana. None of us had ever seen anyone like Burge. He was rail thin with long brown hair and goatee stubble. His eyes were pale grey, and whenever I looked at them it was inadvertent. They were empty and cold. His was the first murder to go to trial in our courthouse in seven years, and the word was that he'd hitchhiked from Des Moines, shown up on a farm about five miles outside of town, and grabbed a chicken from the coop. According to Jan, he broke into the farmhouse, chicken in hand, and walked into the farmer's bedroom. The man was asleep, alone, and Burge slit the chicken's throat and directed the spatter onto his face. When the farmer woke up, Burge treated him to the same fate and then walked the five miles to Hank's Café without even bothering to take a shower. And Hank let him sit there, bloodying up a booth and drinking coffee until the sheriff showed up and charged him right then and there.

At the trial there were newspapermen from Lincoln and Omaha. Jan wore pinstripes and gelled his hair and smiled brightly for their cameras. During recess, he'd come out and stand next to me, and we'd share a cigarette.

"Don't tell anyone," he said once, "But this is open and shut."

In the afternoon, the Priest and Burge would lock eyes. And they'd nod at each other and remain silent while the reporters shouted dozens of simultaneous questions from the bottom of the steps. The Priest didn't offer confession, not during the trial. But that case was the only time he ever stayed past four.

They gave Burge the public defender, and he was foolish enough to put his client on the stand. Burge spoke flatly and muttered to himself, and I've never had a more difficult time recording testimony. At one point he turned his head and glared into the jury box, keeping his eyes focused on the foreman for a solid twenty seconds. Burge was a fearsome man.

After a week, it was over, and we all waited on the steps for a verdict. Jan was cheery and confident, and the public defender napped underneath Lady Justice. Burge wore shackles and cuffs, and when he moved the clanking of metal rang out loud and strong. We all heard him when he walked toward the Priest and sat down, the two of them silent, thinking. The chatter picked up and it was difficult to hear, but I could see the Priest's lips move and thought he said something about absolution. The two of them stood and walked down the stairs, policemen lagging only a step or two behind. When they reached the bottom, the media was frantic, and microphones appeared from all directions. The Priest put up a solemn hand.

"This is between him and God," he said, and his words were followed by a prolonged silence. The flurry of flashes slowed and then ceased. The prattling of reporters and cameramen faded away until there was nothing but a silent crowd, slinking inch by inch away from the steps.

For ten minutes, we all sat watching, staring at the two of them, seated on the bottom step, whispering. The Priest all in black, save for the hint of white at his throat, and Burge clad entirely in orange, carrying metallic accents. It looked like Halloween, like some kind of secret rite, two mysterious, fascinating men conferring and everyone else too afraid to get close.

When they stood up and the Priest took Burge's wrinkled forehead into his palms, we all remained frozen. And when the two broke their ritual embrace and Burge began walking up the steps, there was nothing but more silence, grown heavy and hypnotic. A short woman with dark hair stared at the microphone in her hand, dumbstruck. The Priest began to approach her, and she took a step backward, flinching, forgetting momentarily whatever journalistic instinct had won her a prime spot on KOLN's nightly broadcast. The policemen looked on in horror. Burge strolled past them, calm, peaceful, headed back into court. The Priest continued walking, half-smiling, eyes locked on the woman or maybe her microphone. When he reached her, he stopped.

"My child," he said, "Don't be afraid." The woman looked up, clearly unable to heed his request. Calmly and shakily, she advanced the microphone, bringing it up to his mouth.

"Thank you," he said. "I have forgiven him. In the eyes of God, he is innocent, made pure by His messenger. Let no man undo the work of the Lord."

All the papers said no one could have predicted it. That the verdict was the single largest miscarriage of justice in the history of Custer County. For myself, I'm not sure I can say I disagree. When Jan heard the words, he damn near burst into tears, and when the reporters spoke with him afterward it was difficult to make sense of his meaning amidst the guttural sounds and sobs. The young reporter went back to KOLN and nearly made a career out of the story, spending the next six months running around the country-side reporting on rural superstition and backwoods thinking. I saw her on television last week, when I visited my cousin in Denver. Seems she's done quite well for herself.

Sometime after Jan calmed down, he ran into me at Hank's, and we shared coffee and lemon meringue pie.

"I've been thinking about that priest," he said, and his voice was different, somehow quieter, reflective.

"Yeah, what about him?" I asked.

"How long was it he was out there, would you say? A year? Two?"

"Maybe fifteen months," I said, "Definitely not two."

"And no one's seen him there since, right?"

"Not that I know of."

"I got to wondering," he said, "You remember all those people he talked to before Burge? The shoplifters, the teenage car thieves?"

"Yeah."

"I been thinking I'm not sure any of those juries ever returned a guilty verdict. Thinking maybe this Priest was some kind of charm or something."

I've never been much for conspiracy theories. Most of the time, if you listen hard enough, you can tell everything about a person and their situation just by the sound of their voice and their words on the page. But the more I think about it, the more I think maybe Jan was on to something. Someday, I'd like to find out, tour small-time county courthouses the way some people tour baseball stadiums or national parks. Just pack up the car and ride around until I come upon a baldheaded priest standing guard over the gateway to justice, looking stern and solemn and offering confession to all who pass by. Or maybe there's a better way. A way to plug into the national network of stenographers and see if anyone has some type on the guy. See if maybe one of them was smart enough, or maybe devious enough, to record his staircase conferences like they were official testimony. That would be the way to find out.

After twenty years, you learn to read between the lines. The problem comes when there are no lines to read between. At that point, anything's possible, and you start to imagine the Priest removing that collar every night, laughing to himself in the mirror. You start to imagine him in town after town, and you even start to think about Burge joining him, always similarly charged, each time with a different name. When you live by the record, it's amazing what you'll do when there isn't one. Amazing how quickly rationality fades and is replaced by the most torturous kind of imagination. It's enough to make a man want to write everything down, which everyone in town says is impossible. They say there's too much happening, that no mere mortal could possibly write it all. They could be right, but who's to say, really? Who can know for certain unless some ambitious soul decides to try?

Happy Fish Bait n' Tackle

The guy's name was Mike. He had broad shoulders. We met online. Our first date was supposed to be at the Mulberry's down State 19, but at the last minute he called and said a friend of his had this softball team short players. He said they had a particular need for women, and I don't know why, but maybe I liked his picture. Maybe I knew word traveled and wouldn't Kev be jealous seeing his little Pop-Tart move on so fast. The point is this. I said yes, and we met at the Western Diamonds out past the interstate. He didn't shake my hand or try for a hug or nothing. Just saw me coming up to the dugout and tossed me a glove and a T-shirt and that was that.

Our sponsor was the Happy Fish Bait n' Tackle Shoppe. The shirt was green. It had this goldfish on the front that was smiling like it was stoned. The captain, who I guess Mike knew from the old days, put me in right field, and nothing came my way for five innings, and we were losing 12-1 so that was all we played. I grounded to second twice. Mike was the only guy in the whole place to strike out, and he just looked at me and shrugged. "Oil fields," he said. "Went and messed with my vision, and some days I think it won't ever come back."

We stayed around afterward. There was another game, and we watched and sat in the bleachers and talked. All the men looked like high school football players. Guys who used to lift and bulk up and then got older and wider and never could drop the weight. Mike kept talking about North Dakota. He said the sky was big and the company rough and half his money went to these blackjack tables in nowhere bars or else some women he was embarrassed he chased. That was the old him, he wanted me to know. And didn't make no sense hiding it, but he went and got right with Jesus, and ain't we all sinners too.

When the game ended, they shut the lights off. The parking lot emptied. We watched lightning bugs cut through the humidity and stars over the highway, and I went to pick up cans of Natural Light at the base of the fence. Mike asked me what I thought about God. I said, "I imagine He doesn't much care," and laughed. He said, "I shouldn't be saying this, and I always get myself in trouble, but I'm feeling this sense like He's got something special in mind for you, and all night I been thinking like maybe you'll let me in on it and maybe this is end of the line."

I slapped at a mosquito. I looked in his eyes. They flashed sad and injured and serious, and I threw some aluminum toward the recycling and did my damndest not to panic. To hang in there. To smile in the dark and somehow keep myself from running away.

White Picket Fence

On the way home, I found the baby in the rearview. He was asleep. Wayne was slumping next to him in the back and giving me a look like I should keep my eyes on the road, only I couldn't stop thinking about our chain-link fence. The metal is rusted. In three or four spots it's also coming loose at the top, and I imagined Wayne out there surrounded by pieces of jungle gym. There would be tools on the ground. Beer cans too. He'd be cursing and sometimes lobbing the cans into the alley, calling them home runs or touchdowns as the neighbors tried to fix their cars or maybe listened to the Huskers while raking the leaves. Once in a while, they'd all laugh together above the wind and the rustling and the electric voices, and I'd just be sitting inside with the baby, watching TV and hoping he'd make it in spite of us, that what we were doing was our damned and level best.

Power Left

Best athlete we ever had, that Westhead kid. Wasn't no bigger than you or me but all muscle and hit like napalm. Like cancer. Like he didn't care who you were or if you might be armed. Four-year letterman at fullback and ended up walking on at Nebraska. Dressed all but one game for that '99 team won the Big XII, and that was the one at Texas. Learned their lesson too, I guess, because he was rostered for the rematch, and look how that turned out.

Somebody did an interview with him last week. I forget if it was public TV or ESPN or something else, but they showed parts of it on KMGH. The guy asked him, he said, You're not planning on being at the reunion this Saturday, are you, and Westhead said he didn't do that kind of thing anymore. Knew he'd be the only one and couldn't care less. So, the interviewer, who I guess is a big deal in Kansas City or Chicago or someplace, he asks why. Westhead just looks at him. Looks at him like he's about to snap, or maybe like he's plum sick of answering such a stupid question. Then he takes this deep breath and starts telling a story about staying in Lincoln for summer workouts, about lifting and running stairs and getting so hungry for Mulberry's he gets in his car one night at like eight o'clock. It's this Honda Civic his old man fixed up for him. No A/C and a cracked speaker, and even though it's a couple hundred miles and humid as a hoop house, he ain't stopping until he gets what he needs. So, he drives. He gets to the one in North Platte and figures, fuck it, might as well keep going, and it's a nice night. The stars are out. Semis are flying on past headed back east, but it feels like there's no one else on his side of the freeway, no one else who owns this state like he does. He sings Springsteen to himself the whole way. He rolls down the window and feels moths smash against his forearms like tackling dummies, like practice squad safeties. It's pushing midnight when he pulls up, and the place has the usual crowd of drifters and loonies. Maybe I was there, sitting in a corner booth and watching mosquitoes crawl up the window, I can't remember. He says he thinks he ordered the "Heart Attack Platter," which was new then and sounded dangerous. Maybe he was trying to kill himself, who knows? Maybe he'd already been hit one too many times and was tired of doing all the work for none of the credit. Maybe that's why he was back here, and he says people nodded at him. Like, even the deadbeats who couldn't give a rat's ass about football, they just looked and somehow knew like this guy is special. This guy is something else. They're standing around so reverential he has to autograph like six paper cups, one of which he says is so full of condensation that the ink runs and makes it look like he signed left-handed, before they finally let him out the door with his food. He wants to drive down to the river and eat it there, maybe toss the bag when he's done and watch it float on back to Lincoln and into the Missouri and then the big river, the big American river, and toward Mexico and the Caribbean. Problem is he can't get out of the parking lot. There's a guy standing in front of his car holding the same red, white, and blue bag and just staring. He's got a beard. Has to weigh 250 at least. Westhead says it's clear the guy's on something, and he tries to just walk past him and into his car, but the guy says, You got about a billion dead bugs on your windshield there, buddy, before he can get by. Westhead doesn't make eye contact. He says, Then he tells me for ten bucks he'll read my future, like cast my horoscope from the spatter or something.

And, says the interviewer, What'd you do?

Westhead's got this coy smile. He looks at the camera. There's half a shiner under his left eye. He says, Alls I do is I give him a twenty and tell him I know what's coming. In fact, I can see it a whole lot better than him.

Put a Mask on the Moon

Back when Mom still had her license, she would sometimes moonlight at the hospital in Gothenburg. It was always overnights, and if it was slow or she was on break I'd get calls at three, four in the morning. There would be footsteps echoing steady in the background, like no one was in a rush. She'd tell me about farmers with heartburn, terrified Mexicans holding broken wrists and covering tattoos, these kids that inhaled laundry detergent or drank themselves sick. There was the guy who tried to cut off his pinkie to win a bar bet and then a woman who swore she tripped while sleepwalking and trying to fetch the mail. Most of the time it was fevers and stitches and splints, but once she didn't even bother to say hello. I picked up, and it was just, "Listen, Aims, I'm at the Perkins up 80 with a man named Wayne Weatherby, and he seems nice enough, but there you have it just in case." It didn't sound like a Perkins. More like a bathroom or crowded apartment. Somebody kept imitating a hawk I think, and Mom was either humming or trying to shush.

The next morning, she sat at the kitchen table drinking coffee like nothing happened. It was clear she hadn't slept, and when she handed me a cinnamon roll I said, "These taste like the ones they make down the street."

I remember the way she smiled. How for a second I thought she was going to stand up and pound her fist, maybe slap me across the face. What she ended up doing was sighing. Laughing a little. What she did was put her hands in the air and say, "Look, he was a perfect fucking gentleman, okay? And you'll be happy to know I'll probably never see him again."

A Simple Explanation of Benefits

For health insurance purposes, what is colloquially referred to as "rehab" falls under the category of Drug, Alcohol, and Behavioral Health Services. The Healthcare Common Procedure Coding System (HCPCS) reserves a series of thirty codes, numbered H0001 through H0030, for patient services falling within this category. As is the case with many other medical procedures, a particular bill may contain multiple codes or multiple entries of the same code. H0004, for example, which corresponds to 15 minutes of behavioral health counseling and therapy, will appear four times when a patient, call her Marietta Hollinfell, attends an hour-long, one-on-one session at Heartland Recovery in North Platte, NE. When she attends group therapy, the session will be coded as H0005. Any necessary testing of samples for intoxicants will be H0003, and the entire 30-day, residential treatment program will fall under H0018 (which does not include room and/or board and which any experienced coder will tell you must be listed once per day (so 30 times in total) on any subsequent EOB or billing statement). None of this includes the initial assessment or screening to which Ms. Hollinfell will have to submit in order to be eligible for any residential treatment program, experiences which might be coded as H0001 or H0002, depending. Ms. Hollinfell will be glad to know, however, that these pre-program steps are likely to enjoy more insurance coverage thanks to legal requirements introduced as part of the Affordable Care Act, though specifics will of course vary depending on her particular insurance plan, and, in fact, while many codes falling within the scope of the Drug, Alcohol, and Behavioral Health Services category are subject to the standard rules regarding deductibles and out-of-pocket maximums, policy terms are sometimes written in such a way as to define what constitutes an acceptable H0018 (just for example) narrowly, which often results in unexpected expenses. Given that Ms. Hollinfell has a plan from a UnitedHealthcare subsidary (called UnitedHealthOne) obtained through her employer, a florist just off I-80 on the far western edge of North Platte, it's likely she'll have one such policy. This means that her EOBs for the initial steps of the process (namely the screening and evaluation), which, it should be noted, may not arrive until after her completion of the full, 30-day program, will appear minimal, and this may lead to an assumption on her part that the entire process will enjoy similar coverage (or perhaps that the initial payment she will have no trouble making will cover the entire experience, even though there are other billing statements en route). Of course, she'll be warned by news stories and nurses about cost, and Heartland itself will walk her through its billing procedures with an explicit warning that coverage may vary, a warning she'll largely ignore, perhaps out of ignorance or laziness but just as likely because she's exhausted and desperate and still a little high, so that even on Day 5, when she will, for the first time in maybe 18 months, feel genuine emotion (primarily shame, but also an intense burst of empathy for a 44-year-old former nurse named Nadelle, a member of her cohort who will share a story about being so zoned on oxy that she ran over her daughter's cat (a Russian Blue they called Pavel after a character in a Willa Cather novel) on her way to a family dinner), she will already have run up a substantial debt. The H0004s, H0005s, and H0018s will all be logged, tabulated, and sent on a rolling basis to a UHC claims processor working in Minnetonka, MN, who will compare them with Ms. Hollinfell's policy, generate a billing statement for review, and save a digital copy that will be accessible from anywhere via UHC database but stored on a server at a $100 million data center in Chaska. This digital record is what will be called up by Joseph, a call center rep in Chandler, AZ, when Ms. Hollinfell's uncle, Apex, dials the customer service number listed on the relevant insurance card (Marietta herself being practically hungover from detox and sticker shock (to the point that, when the bill arrives, she'll attend five separate meetings over the course of 36 hours)). Apex will have brushed up on insurance lingo via online videos and web articles, but he'll be no match for Joseph, who (as soon as he senses the tension rise) will transfer him to Kay in Kansas City, claiming that she'll have a much better grasp of the particularities of UHC's Nebraska operation. She won't, of course, but she'll pretend to, projecting an air of competence and Midwestern politeness throughout the conversation, about halfway through which Apex will lose all control (and call her a "useless bitch"), though this won't bother Kay, who'll just ask if he wants to speak to a supervisor and send him right on through when he agrees. The phone will ring and ring and no one will answer, though it's possible a Consumer Redirection Assistance System (CRAS) will eventually send him to a voicemail for a Lydia Jones, Staff Supervisor for General Claims, where he'll leave a frustrated, profanity-laced message that will be routinely cleared out at the end of the month by either an intern or first-year consumer rep. Now, Apex (being a bit stubborn) may call back, and maybe he'll get through to someone who authorizes a discount, or maybe he'll start taking shots during the nonstop hold music (which will be an old Bach concerto intercut with a deep, African-American male voice talking about UHC's record of innovation and customer satisfaction), but most people won't go that far. For most people, it will end right there. UHC will get its money somehow (even if it isn't Marietta who ends up paying it), and, though rank-and-file employees may occasionally reflect on the morality of all this, the economy will grow and share prices will rise, and the market itself will have no real cause for complaint.

3rd

Quarter

Lincoln Highway Jesus

On our second date, Mike took me to his church. The building looked abandoned. It was between the Bomgaars and the bowling alley, and on the way inside he told me this wasn't a permanent spot, that they met somewhere different every week. The preacher, who everyone called Lightning or Lightning Bug, would announce the next location at the end of each service. They didn't use email. Sometimes, somebody would volunteer to hand out flyers. "The idea is to keep it small," Mike said, "Keep it chosen." And word would spread through flaming tongues or the grace of the Holy Spirit.

"Like the early Christians," I said, and he looked at me like I was some kind of genius, or maybe like I was from outer space.

The sermon was about agriculture. We could see plants and seed bags and rusted pickups out the window. Lightning Bug said he'd just read an article about erosion, and the author guessed that, in places like Iowa and Nebraska, we had maybe only 80 or 100 harvests left. After that it would be starvation and pain and complete food system collapse. He said he stayed up real late, and if you wanted a picture of what it might be like, all you had to do was watch one of them commercials for UNICEF or the Red Cross or whatever it was, and there would be a lot of ribcages and a lot of flies, and no one would have the energy to swat them away.

I looked around, and people had their eyes closed. Some of them were nodding a little. It was hard to tell if they'd fallen asleep. Lightning said he didn't know what to make of the article, except he kept thinking about pride, which was really arrogance, which we all knew was a deadly sin. He said maybe the author was arrogant. After all, the ways of God are a mystery, and the signs you're reading may not be meant for you. Then again, if the author was right, then we were arrogant. We'd spent the last hundred years wasting His gifts. Mike shouted at that. Everyone else seemed to agree. Then, Lightning Bug said there was only one lesson to draw, and it was about the future and our utter lack of control. He said comeuppance was in the air. Comeuppance was real. Comeuppance was coming, and we were all sinners, and every last sinner would get his justified due.

Platte River Love Song

The night after the election, me and Adler went fishing. There were these two girls with us. I don't remember where we got them, probably The Buffalo Horn or Campfire Joe's, but the one was skinny with black hair and the other had on this raspberry perfume that made her smell like a teenager. Maybe she was, but she looked 29 at the very least. We went to this spot he knew out past Cozad with a case of High Life and about a dozen hot dogs from the Dairy Queen. It was windy, and the black-haired girl kept laughing and throwing empty cans overboard until Adler told her to "show some goddamn respect."

"Respect this," she said, and lobbed a hot dog toward the front of the boat. He caught it and nodded a kind of thanks. I said, "We used to know this guy Matt who loved these things. Would eat six at a time." We told them how, once, when the Huskers were at Texas, we dared him to eat one for every point, and by the end of the game he'd had 20.

"What happened to him?" the one with the perfume wanted to know. She meant that day, but we just looked at each other and shrugged.

We talked for a while about the wind and Bruce Springsteen and Charles Starkweather. You could hear water hitting the boat, and every time we caught a sunny we threw it into the Dairy Queen bag, on top of about four cans of beer. It would make a sound like a hockey puck, or else gravel spraying your hubcaps. The girls thought we should let them go, but Adler said if you do it for one, you got to do it for all, and they pretended to understand.

I didn't feel like fucking, but Adler did, and me and perfume ferried him and skinny back to shore. I think they did it in the truck, and he must've turned the ignition to ACC because the Ultimate Johnny Cash Collection started playing while we hung near the weeds and looked at the stars and drank. She was on her fifth High Life by then, on top of whatever she took before we met, so she kept belching over the side of the boat and trying to talk politics. Most of it was nonsense. At some point, I told her the only thing that mattered was the death penalty repeal, and that was all I voted for because it was a lost cause anyway. She seemed to take offense. Stood up like she was going to hit me, or maybe like she wanted to dance, and it sent the nose forward enough we almost hit water. I grabbed her shoulder and said I was sorry. She closed her eyes, and I put my arm around her waist, and we fell toward the river with me trying to kiss her, thinking maybe that might set the world back straight.

The Grand Finale

For the Fourth, Dad let us take the camper out to Creekside. He gave us a case of High Life and a box of Roman candles and said we were old enough to be treated like men. To make our own fun. Clark said he probably just wanted to let Audrey run around in her panties for a day or two, but I didn't care, and we grabbed the keys and hardly looked back.

The case didn't survive the night. Clark had 16, and I had 8, and halfway through he said we should drive to that missile silo out near Lodgepole and act like it was the end of the world, and so we unhitched the Chevy, and that's exactly what we did. We brought a lighter and the fireworks. It was cloudy, and there wasn't no moon, and we heard about a million moths, but neither of us could see shit. We parked maybe 50 feet down the road and sat inside the truck for a while, talking about bomb shelters and canned goods and how many batteries you'd need to run a microwave for life. I said I'd kill to bring Kelly from the Dairy Queen down there with me, but Clark didn't think you wanted women. He said you'd be better off just having a few on film and then listed off some names I can't remember, except for one that might have been Laramie Voyeur. I said that would eat into your battery supply pretty quick, but what I meant was things might get lonely, and then Clark opened the door and went to line up a few candles across from the fence. He put them in beer bottles, and I told him he was crazy. That I didn't think he was serious, and there were probably cameras, and this was federal prison and big, Black guys from Arkansas type shit. He didn't listen. Just kept right on lighting fuses and then sprinted his way back to the truck.

It started smooth, and he gunned it. Gravel hit the hubcaps. Flares came up in the rearview. He pushed it to 90, and the lights faded behind us, and we hit the interstate and figured we'd made it for good. Bruce came on the radio. Clark was saying how those cameras ain't have night vision, and you know the truck's in Dad's name too. I tried to picture barium or strontium or phosphorous. Then, it was two miles later, and I wondered why we weren't singing along.

Stars and Stripes Forever

A few years back, one of the Sorensen kids made a documentary. It was about this adjunct in Communication over at UNL, this guy named George Anthony Sims. Wasn't much interesting about him that I can recall, except that he fancied himself some kind of crusader and got this idea one day while reviewing a speech about 9/11 or the invasion of Iraq or something that he was going to start wearing an American flag pin to his classes and around the office. He changes nothing else. Same office hours, same routine, same wardrobe (featuring blue jeans and blazers in assorted colors), same everything. Only difference is now there's the Stars & Stripes pinned right there on his lapel, and it ain't obvious but it ain't exactly discreet neither. That sort of thing was everywhere around that time, maybe you remember. There were rainbows and purple ribbons, paper clips and safety pins, these little signs saying "we love our neighbors" in Spanish. They were on office doors and bulletin boards and pretty well all across campus, and, the filmmaker, she fills us in on all this with photos and interviews from experts and commentators, all of whom say basically the same thing. The point was to communicate openness. To show the "marginalized members of the community, quickly and instantly, that they were welcome and supported."

Sims had nothing against any of that. Right there on camera, he says the whole thing was basically just an experiment, and his own hypothesis (which we should note is documented nowhere other than the film itself) was that no one would even notice, and, if they did, the reaction would be either muted or nonexistent. Turns out, of course, he was dead wrong, and wouldn't be much of a movie otherwise. Chatter starts up almost instantly. He overhears colleagues talking in the break room, the hallway, to students in the offices next door. Some of them roll their eyes when he walks by. Attendance rates in his rhetorical theory classes start to drop, and a few students file reports alleging a "bias incident" or else some form of discrimination. The phrase "hate speech" gets thrown around on social media and starts popping up in discussion groups and campus-wide emails, and it gets bad enough that, about three weeks in, Sims is burned in effigy in front of the union. It's pretty clear his contract isn't going to be renewed, and the only complicating factor is that, right around the same time, a small group of students starts wearing the flag too. At first, it's just the College Republicans, but soon you've got kids from all over the state, from York to Kearney to Ogallala (mostly men and mostly angry (some even justifiably)), and there are rallies and anti-rallies, protests and counter-protests. The administration starts sending out these missives full of various forms of hedging and openly suggests banning all such pins and paraphernalia, only to piss the hell out of everyone and back off almost immediately. There are panels on "civil discourse." Discussions in humanities classes (and the film says nothing about what happened in math or biology or computer science, but my assumption was that they probably couldn't be bothered) get real heated, and pretty soon tenured faculty are doing little but complaining about the uncontrollable nature of their classrooms. The whole environment is poison, they say (citing examples of shouting matches and fist pounds and aggressions both macro and micro, not to mention the complete deterioration of anything resembling a coherent argument (which, Sims takes pleasure in pointing out, "most of these tenured assholes wouldn't recognize if it was stated in plain English on an eye chart")), and some of them start cursing Sims to his face, while others refer to him obliquely in faculty meetings as a "revolutionary" or "provocateur" or "iconoclast" (or directly as a "fascist"). He gets death threats, it should go without saying. Some of them are colorful, and some of them are boring, and the film shows a collage of his personal favorites (including one that says, "Why burn a flag when you can burn the Nazi wrapped in it?") that now hangs in his new office because, by the end, he's relocated and become either the head of something at the Cato Institute or else is teaching at Hillsdale and on the fastest track to tenure the college allows (and maybe you've read something of his in *The Federalist* or watched him on *Newsmax*), and I can't recall which.

The film didn't make much of a splash. Everyone turned it down except for one of the streaming services (which now shows it for free and with commercials and probably only to people really willing to look), but the director did an interview with the local paper, and they asked her what she wanted viewers to take from it. Mostly, she played it coy. She said she hopes it makes them think. She said she hopes they realize we live in the land of opportunity, and everyone tries to take advantage.

Dawson County Postcards

In October, Pike found half a deer on the side of Country Club Road. It was the back half. I said the front was probably rotting away somewhere in all that corn out there, but Adler thought it must've got itself carried off by a band of crows. It smelled a little. All the blood was dry. Pike stood the thing up on its hind legs and then stripped down and leaned what was left of it against his naked ass. We made jokes about maggots. Pinworms. Adler said they'd crawl out in the middle of night and scare some dark-haired bar rat half to death, and she'd scream loud enough to wake that old drunk from all the way down the block.

Pike told us to shut up and take the pictures. That his balls were freezing, and he had plans, and there wasn't much light left anyway. I used his phone. I said, way back when, you couldn't've had these printed without some clerk calling the cops, or at least thinking you were a perv. Pike laughed. Except the problem with self-service, said Adler, is in this case the clerk was like to call you after, on account of that right there would be the biggest one she'd ever seen. With Pike's luck the clerk would be a guy, I said, and then we talked about Minna. Minna his ex-wife. Minna who sold pickled vegetables and said they'd survive nuclear winter. Last 150 years and outlive cockroaches, and then she moved way down to El Paso with some Mexican, or maybe he was an Indian, and, in any case, he used to order these great big cases of her stuff through the mail. We figured the whole thing was some kind of plan to win her back or maybe make her see what she was missing, but when I asked what she'd do when she got the pictures, Pike said he might not even send them at all. Adler called him a motherfucker. I said, then what was the goddamn point, and he looked at us like we had no eyes and practically shoved us into the car. We drove back toward Campfire Joe's, and after a while he said, you boys ain't know nothing about healing, and this shit here's what you call a little memento, it's what you call the last resort.

Guerilla Marketing

The night the death penalty repeal failed, a 23-year-old marketing staffer wrote to one of the VPs. It was after midnight. The prose reads rushed. Almost drunk. There are no apostrophes and barely any commas. This kid's name was Heron, and he said he'd only been working at Mulberry's for six months, but he was a Communication major at Kearney, and one of his courses talked extensively about immersive marketing and potential growth areas for edgy brands. Here was the idea. The first inmate slated for execution post-reinstatement was a guy named Matthew Alan Nowinski, and this kid had it on good authority that Nowinski loved Mulberry's. They were both from Dawson County. He said he knew Nowinski's cousin or a friend of his old girlfriend or maybe a couple of guys he liked to watch the Huskers with back in the day, and whoever it was told him that the guy used to drive all the way to Ogallala (this being back before we opened the North Platte or Kearney locations, the kid said) for Weasel burgers and Cajun Pepper fries. He would dip everything in ranch dressing, and it was a good bet, according to everything he'd heard, that this Nowinski was going to request some version of that for his last meal. Now, the kid understood the risks here, and he could anticipate objections a mile away. But given the place's general ethos and commitment to pushing the advertising envelope (and just look at what we did with that E. coli. thing back in the 90s), he thought maybe they'd want to take the opportunity to turn the whole thing into branded content of some sort (by offering financial incentives (to be distributed to Nowinski's family, or at least the closest relatives we can find, of course) to ensure he goes with us), and think of the payoff. The danger, the allure, the influx of new customers and social media commentary. He said he'd run point if it came to that, and his vision involved targeted online communication. Posts on message boards and comment threads and all the microblogging services, with emphasis placed on societal fringes. He wanted to sell "The Nowinski" for the month leading up to the scheduled date of execution, only it wouldn't be on the menus. You'd have to ask for it like it was Prohibition (and if you did it the week of, maybe we could even make it free). Like you were entering a speakeasy, and, after you mentioned it, the clerk would say something like "Try to Control Yourself" or "Long Live the King" before ringing up your food. He imagined people coming from miles away. Making little Mulberry's pilgrimages. Writing Twitter travelogues and posting photos of themselves with grease-stained bags. They'd be holding up these plastic cups of ranch and sticking their tongues out, maybe pretending their necks were in nooses or else like a needle was about to go in. It would be big, he said, and, in his opinion, well worth any potential fallout because think of it. The only people who would notice would be the ones in on the joke, and they weren't likely to criticize, were they? Not to mention the national media's ignored Nebraska for years, and no one trusts them anyway (and are we really afraid anyone local might sniff this out?), so what's the point of playing it safe? Because even if they do notice, they're only gonna talk about us more, and anger fuels sales, and, at the end of the day, the kid said he was okay with being fired. The suggestion was worth it. He didn't take the job not to say what he meant (and that's what you bastards taught me to do, and I gotta say, you did a damn fine job).

The funny thing is, it doesn't seem like any of the hedging was necessary. The internal memos and rejoinders from other VPs and even the C-Suite were all enthusiastic. At some point, someone will leak the emails, and you'll be able to see for yourself. Fuck yeah, wrote one of the women in R&D. A few of them traded jokes about market penetration and being too hot for TV. The VP of Marketing & Public Relations said he deserved a bonus for putting in place the protocols that led to the hiring of someone so obvious-ly bold, so goddamn brilliant, and can we start right now, which is what they agreed to do. Heron was promoted immediately. Projec-tions called for a 30-percent increase in fourth-quarter profits, and that turned out to be conservative. The whole thing came off per-fectly, and, immediately after the execution, the Public Relations team, in conjunction with Heron himself (with additional input from a group of hired consultants), put out a press release. It read as follows: "Matthew Alan Nowinski's last supper was a Double Wea-sel burger, an extra-large order of Cajun Pepper fries, and four sides of ranch dressing. Our thoughts go out to the victims and their families, as well as to everyone impacted by Mr. Nowinski's crimes. It is our intention to donate 10 percent of all purchases from now until the end of the year to victims' advocacy services and local law enforcement, and it's our desire to be a unifying force within the community. As always, we are grateful for your support. We look forward to continuing our unparalleled tradition of service to the people of Nebraska and to fulfilling our integral role in the good life of our great state."

Neighbors

We had a guy back at the old place. Lived like three, four houses down. Eddie was his name. Tall. A little paunchy. Had a laugh like an electric drill. You could hear it from halfway down the block sometimes, like if you were out for a walk and he had his windows open because it was a nice night. A woman lived with him, I think, but I never saw a wedding band, and we all came to the conclusion that it wasn't no formal thing. We liked the guy. Or I did anyway. Maxine thought he was a little twitchy, but wasn't no harm to him. Not really. When we tell the story now, I think of it like a bumper sticker. Like an easy way to explain why we lit out when we did, left a house we loved and moved two towns over, with longer commutes and new schools for the kids. After a couple beers I sometimes tell Maxine we were crazy to go through the hassle, but she's sure we made the only choice we could. "But Caleb's got three C's this term," I say, "And Anna, why last time she talked to me about anything other than can-I-borrow-the-car had to be six months ago, maybe more." "Better that than dead," she says, and I want to say she's being a fucking loony, but who needs it when it's all past mattering. When she's always, usually right.

What happened was Eddie made a fuss one night. Stood out on his porch eight or ten drinks deep and yelling at the whole neighborhood. Talking about health insurance companies or some corporation owns the slaughterhouse where he works, this place up halfway to Broken Bow. Couldn't have been much past 7:30, and there's Eddie screaming and ranting and setting off fireworks until the cop pulls up. I can still see him walking to the door. Young kid. Couldn't've been much past 22. Anyway, he does the usual thing.

Got some complaints, sir. Why don't you go on back inside and let these people have some peace? Dogs are barking like you wouldn't believe, and that was always the worst part of the old neighborhood. Dogs jumping at you from every corner and looking half-starved. Pit bulls, mostly. Mangy fuckers with sharp eyes and negligent owners way worse than ol' Eddie. Eddie wouldn't hurt a fly. But he tells the officer he's a man to be feared, and he flies off the handle a little. Says things shouldn't never be said, at least not out loud, and not in front of the Law. Says he's gonna commit one of them mass shootings, and he's got a basement full of hunting rifles, and they can be rigged for much, much worse. The officer sighed, I remember. Didn't panic or nothing. Just reached for his radio. About then was when Eddie's woman came running out. Wearing like gym shorts and a Springsteen T-shirt and saying how wasn't no gun in the house at all and the officer could come have a look if he liked. Got coffee too, she said, and the whole time is pulling Eddie back and rubbing his arm a little like you-better-behave-you-ever-want-to-touch-me-again. She said something about a rough couple of days and gave the officer a look that said "trust me" and "you don't want to know." They talked for a while. The kid cop said something into his radio. Five minutes or so go by. All parties get a little calmer. Another cruiser pulls up, and the kid goes inside with a lady cop looked much more experienced. The two of them come back after maybe 10 or 15, and they only got Eddie's woman with them. They look sympathetic. Like they're apologizing even, and then they all shake hands, and the cops get in their cruisers and drive away, and it all seems like no big deal. Neighborhood talks for a while, but nothing comes back to Eddie, not that we can see, and if it weren't for that look in Maxine's eyes, I would have chalked it up to just another one of those things.

I haven't heard anything about Eddie since we left. Haven't bothered to look. Don't know if he got liver cancer or a new woman or made the trip to Lincoln for the Iowa game. But I think of him sometimes at the grocery store. I look at them frozen packages of meat and picture Eddie with a knife. Eddie with blood on his boots. Eddie smoking on break and then showing his boss his ass on the way out the door. Then, I go home and throw on some coals. I smell the ash and look out at my lawn and open a beer. Anna starts the car. Caleb's inside shooting Nazis or Russians and shouting at friends he's never met. The TV is loud enough to wake the dead. Maxine will be home in 20, and there won't be a reason to mention Eddie because it will only start a fight, and, anyway, that poor fucker is probably a long way gone.

Aural Sex

We drove past corn and prairie grass and under these bridges made to look like covered wagons. Tom found the Vivid channel on satellite radio, and we listened to two women discussing blow-job techniques at full volume. Their stage names were Nova and Laramie. One of them sounded Mexican and more attractive, and Tom said we wouldn't believe it, but he met her once, back last year at a Subway in Winnetka because, he didn't know if we knew, but that was where she grew up. He said he wasn't out looking for her or anything. She had on sweatpants and a Bears jersey and ordered the Cold Cut Combo in this way that made him laugh out loud. He covered his mouth and said a quick prayer she didn't hear. The idea was to act normal. To be a gentleman while seeming dangerous and charming and in that way making an impression, and he also paid for her food. Just kind of edged past her while she asked for extra pickles and gave the cashier six ones and a quarter, blindly hoping it would be enough. Thankfully, it was. I asked if she smiled. Rob wanted to know if he got her number, and he told us she didn't say a word. I said that was probably a blessing. In the car, her voice was leather and citric and detailed, and we couldn't imagine the pain of hearing it for real. Rob wondered if maybe we could turn it off now please, and in the back I sort of half-nodded while Tom told us, listen, if this doesn't get you charged up, I can pull this car over right here, and you two assholes can hitchhike the whole rest of the way.

Brand New Man

I heard about a guy out near Pleasanton (or maybe it was Prairie Center) who didn't leave his house for a year. It might have been even longer. The whole thing was some kind of publicity stunt or radical experiment to see how long he could go without in-person contact, and he originally wanted to attract sponsors and livestream the entire experience, but the only businesses he could convince were RuralRoutes (a company specializing in high-speed internet access and fiber infrastructure in remote areas) and Mulberry's (which supplied him with Weasel burgers and Monkey fries and all the fish sandwiches he could eat). There were concerns about brand identity and the potential for negative association. He ended up broadcasting only discrete moments, and you could, for example, watch him unloading groceries (picked up at the Walmart in Kearney (by independent contractors he hired off Craigslist) and then (according to previously agreed upon instructions) left on the porch) or doing P90X in an unfinished basement (something that occurred with regularity and at all hours, always with hardcore metal playing in the background, and it was occasionally loud enough that the neighbors would hear the bass vibrating (or else what they described as "screechy little echoes") and think about calling the cops, though, in the end, they never did, maybe because they were afraid or maybe because they didn't want to be rude). Sometimes he would exchange texts with friends or talk to family via Skype (which, of course, was not an official sponsor), and the conversation varied depending on the audience. With some he talked about this sort of content analysis he was doing on the varieties of internet pornography (for which he was working on a "revolutionary new rating algorithm"), and with others he would reminisce about Husker teams from the 90s (whose rosters he'd memorized while watching and re-watching highlight videos and archived games). He might mention a newly developed devotion to Mexican League soccer (and Chivas in particular) or else his progress on Spanish vocabulary or a sudden inability to read anything longer than four pages (perhaps noting one or two pieces of short fiction that made some marginal impact), but the one constant was his description of the totality of it. He didn't miss anyone, he said. Was in the best shape of his life. In fact, he felt like he knew more about the modern world than anyone ever could, and he wanted to just keep on doing what he was doing forever, and why the hell not? Maybe he'd go ahead and die there, and maybe no one would notice, and wouldn't that be the best way to go?

At first, the person listening would think he was deep into some kind of bad trip or cabin fever dream, but then he'd take a minute to think. He'd talk to a friend. He'd do some introductory analysis on comparative levels of pleasure and say to himself, You know. This crazy bastard might actually be right.

A Rising Tide

One year, the Platte got so high whole neighborhoods had to be evacuated. People lit out for the hills or else got discounted rates on hotel rooms near the highway (where families pretended it was a vacation and their kids said (probably without meaning it) that they never wanted to go back home). In the trailer parks, hundreds of folks stayed behind, and even after the river crested they plodded through their kitchens in rain boots and trash bags, trying to feed themselves and also save what could be saved. A hopeful story went around, and it was about a man named Morton who built his trailer out of balsa wood, and they said the water just picked it right up and carried him away (which, of course, meant he didn't have to worry about lot rent or NFIP payouts (something no one was confident in receiving (and certainly not in a timely manner)) and could just enjoy baked beans and High Life and then gaze out the window like it was the lazy river or else some kind of Viking cruise).

It got bad enough that they set up supply checkpoints and then sent the governor in to make a speech. He stood on a stage at a park in Hall County. Mulberry's donated Weasel burgers and Cajun Pepper fries, and staffers (who dressed like volunteers) tossed T-shirts and TP and bottled water to the crowd. The governor (wearing work boots and a Husker (trucker) hat) said most politicians would say they were sad to be here under such circumstances, and, pardon his language, but the truth was that these "circumstances" made him real damn proud. First, he thanked local businesses. He singled out Mulberry's by name. Then, he told a story about an elderly woman who lost everything (and he mentioned her wedding photos and a beloved Golden Retriever named Liberty) and still came up and welcomed him, shook his hand and asked if there was anything she could do. He said he could stand up on this stage and make promises about aid and solidarity, and, yes, the state would do all it could to help. The real comfort, though, was what was already happening. What had been going on since the water hit ground. He said, I'll do everything I can, but it's no match for what you can do for each other, what your local infrastructure has already done. Donations keep coming and neighbors keep helping, and if there's one thing I know, it's that government is here, but Huskers don't need it. And a moment like this lifts all Nebraskans up.

Just About Broke

The commercial opens at a Mulberry's. It's the original, the one in Ogallala (which was, back then, I'm pretty sure the only one there was), and it's practically deserted except for a mother and her son, who's probably about six. They're eating Weasel burgers and Cajun Pepper fries. The whole thing is supposed to have really happened, is based on a real and honest-to-God true story, and the two of them are sitting there talking about how some coyote went and got one of their calves, and all of a sudden you can hear one howling in the background, a coyote. They cut to a shot of him sniffing around the dumpster in the parking lot. It's dark outside, and the restaurant is on fire with neon, and so it all looks shadowed and criminal, but you can tell what's going on. He wants food scraps. He's going to chase off some raccoons.

The mother (whose name in the script is Toni (though this never gets mentioned)) looks at her son. Then she gets up and walks out the door and around the corner, and you can see her through the window. She's in the parking lot, over by the dumpsters too. She's digging in her jacket. She pulls out a concealed carry, and the boy (and he looks like he might be Asian, like he's either adopted or else maybe just kind of deeply tan) runs to the window. He starts tapping on the glass. What are you doing, Mom, he says, and it's all whiny and high-pitched because the poor kid's worked up and hyperventilating and one hundred percent ready to cry. The mom cocks the pistol. The coyote's still sniffing around the trash, and it looks like he's tucked into the remnants of somebody's Heart Attack Platter, and then the night manager's by the window next to the little boy and yelling about how ma'am you can't do that here, and we're in city limits, and don't you know they got these things called laws? Mom looks at the guy through the glass. The kid actually is crying now, you can tell, and her voice comes through muffled but it's only on account of the window, and she says, this motherfucker (or maybe it was son of a bitch, and the thing only aired late at night and mostly got watched on the relatively early internet, so no one much cared about the FCC) or his brother or cousin cost me money, and me and my boy right there just had to leave a calf in a cornfield for the hawks to pick apart, and you don't seem like the type to go ratting nobody out. The manager nods at that. He says, well, then you do what you have to, but don't wait for no more customers because you know how some secrets get that much harder to keep. No, screams the kid, in that campy and drawn-out cinematic way, but the mom just looks right at him. She's in her 40s. Her face is a little broken and leather and sexy, and she tells him, she says, Son, some lessons gotta be learned, and some laws was made to be broke.

The last shot hangs there for a second. The coyote is snarling and walking toward the mom, and she's got the pistol extended but is otherwise all eyes on her son. We see her start to squeeze the trigger, and then all sound cuts out. Screen goes black. All we can see is Mulberry's. And then below it, how it says Try to Control Yourself, and most people couldn't. They gave the place their money, and you ask anyone, what they'll tell you is that little ad brought a nothing prairie franchise all the whole way back.

48 Quit

MacDonald didn't show up to practice, so, when it was over, Coach Bradley met with his Defensive Coordinator in the west end zone. The sun was setting behind them. They each had a beer. Technically, drinking wasn't allowed on school property, but the field had cleared out, and Bradley'd been there for going on 30 years, and that meant he pretty much had the run of the place. He could do whatever he liked.

"Griner said he quit," said the head coach. "Didn't even bother to tell no one. Just left his whole team in the lurch no qualms."

"Soft," said the DC. "Soft, soft, soft."

"Any softer he'd have a thread count."

"He'd be velvet."

"In the old days, they'd a kicked his ass just for thinking about it. Wouldn't even need to get us involved. Just drove him on out to one of them missile silos in the middle of the night and whap whap whap."

"Offered to give him a ride home after too. Long as he didn't cry in the backseat."

"And he wouldn't have neither. Not back then."

"Got that right, and ain't it the truth of it. They don't make them like they did, do they? You always hear it, and now it's like every day there's another sign." The beer they were drinking was High Life. The DC was half done with his.

"They don't even make them in the same tier you ask me. You remember Westhead? Were you here then? So many damn years, I can't remember."

"Westhead was my first and second year. Or third maybe. What a killer. A goddamn monster."

"I never seen a rhino."

"Nope."

"Not up close."

"Me neither."

"But that Westhead was the closest thing to it."

"The hit he put on what's-his-name? Jenkins? Only Black kid in the whole Panhandle had to be. Played a couple years D-3, maybe, up in Minnesota. Christ, I have nightmares about it."

"Put him in the hospital." Bradley half-turned and squinted toward the sun.

"MacDonald never hit a kid like that."

"Got Robard a little woozy a couple weeks ago in practice, but that wasn't nothing, and looked to me like Robard hit the ground a whole lot harder than MacDonald hit him."

"Whereas that Jenkins. Jenkins didn't walk for a month the way I remember it."

"And then still came back to kick our tails the next year, didn't he? Doctors couldn't keep his ass away. And ol' Westhead kept on hitting like a truck, like napalm, no guilt and not a goddamn second thought."

"Not then anyway."

"Not then."

"These days, different story."

"Went soft, didn't he?"

"Went hippie."

"Sold out for the snatch."

"Must've been. Can't think of no other reason."

"You know he's in Wyoming now. Or Utah. Someplace they probably don't even have football, and I can't even look at the son of a bitch when he shows up on TV or what have you. Pops his head up to talk some psychobabble and then goes back to his sheep farm or whatever it is. Hell, maybe he sold out for the sheep."

They both laughed. "Our biggest success and disappointment all at once," said the DC.

"Nah, Lincoln must have been what fucked him up. You and I ain't have nothing to do with it."

"I'll drink to that." The DC raised his beer. Bottles clinked. A few crickets responded. "MacDonald, on the other hand. What is it we're gonna do about MacDonald?"

"You know I'm gonna call his father is what I'm gonna do," said the head coach, "Quitting's one thing, but walking out's another."

"Old man's tough like leather too, ain't he? You know what the kid said to me once? Said, my old man won't send no hog off to slaughter beats him in a wrestling match. No joke. Said he does it like a ritual. Makes the kids take photos, and the ones that beat him, they get their picture hung in this shrine out near the barn. Hay and mud and put out to stud for the rest of their life, and over the years there's been maybe two he can remember, and ain't that about as Husker as it gets right there?"

"If it ain't a bald-faced lie."

"Think so?"

"Either that or the apple fell way off the wrong damn tree, I'll say that."

"Think he'll convince the kid to come back?"

"No. And even if he did, we ain't want him back now, do we? Not like that."

"No."

"Besides the old man's the reflective type. Military man. I got an inkling what he might say."

"What's that?"

"He'll say, 'Coach, I always believed a real man makes his own choices. And some of them choices end up mistakes. And some of them mistakes he learns to regret for a long, long time.'"

They toasted with the last of the beer, making sure not to spill any of it in the end zone. The turf was painted bright red. It caught twilight. It was the most beautiful thing either of them had ever seen.

4th

Quarter

Public Access

They opened the new stadium in early August. The humidity had just broken, and it was 81 degrees, and we came towing blankets and children and footballs. There must have been a hundred of us, or maybe three, or maybe half the town. Tickets were two dollars apiece. Somebody'd put a sheet over the scoreboard, and the CEO of Mulberry's stood at the 50-yard line and pulled a string after the band played the school song. The sheet came down. Balloons flew into the air. We saw a small Jumbotron that said, "Mulberry's welcomes YOU to YOUR Municipal Stadium," and the superintendent gave a speech about pride and togetherness and the virtues only Huskers understood. Afterwards, some people bought Husker Hot Dogs and popcorn. I remember the whole place smelled like grease and bug spray and propane. The kids kept running fly patterns, and footballs would collide in the air. Some were real, and some were soft and neon orange, and after a while there were no quarterbacks and no receivers, and it was like a juggler with dozens of limbs and no sense of order, and we laughed and dodged and caught and tossed.

We stayed until late. Around 8:30, they turned the lights on, and the end zones were so red it looked like the Rose Bowl, and we dove across goal lines and picked rubber pellets out of our guts. Kids jumped on top of us. Our wives watched from the sidelines. Some of them took pictures, and a few just looked away. Before the place closed, we laid on our backs and saw gnats swarming. Heard cars flying by on the interstate. We told ourselves we pitied them. That we wouldn't trade places, not for a second, and, wherever they're going, it can't be nearly this good.

Capacities of Self-Abuse: An Ethno-, Porno-Graphic Immersion

By the time he was a third-year grad student, Larry Baskin knew that if he ever hoped to be recognized as any kind of authority on the hegemonic American male, he would have to study either football or pornography, and, since he had no real taste for violence (though there were several (mainly feminist) future scholars in his cohort who claimed that there was violence present in even the most culturally acceptable forms of pornography and argued, occasionally rather convincingly, that its sexualized nature made it even more dangerous than its gridiron counterpart), the latter seemed like the only available choice. At first (as he would have readily admitted), his research was quite limited, focusing entirely on masturbation rituals and pornographic viewing habits among heterosexual, U.S. males, aged 18-29. Relying primarily on anonymized survey data (from participants asked to take part in a series of studies on "sexual health") and more in-depth personal interviews, Baskin collected information about factors ranging from masturbatory duration to type of material used (e.g. photos, video or audio files (accessed either digitally or via physical copy, though, across all cohorts, the digital method was much-preferred), individually imagined (or lived and "replayed") experiences, etc.) to ejaculate receptacles (some of which included socks, toilet paper, Kleenex (and there was one participant who said he preferred to use the boxes rather than the tissues), old T-shirts, etc.), eventually cataloguing what he called (in conference presentations and cover letters for job applications (mostly addressed to middling state universities with second-(or third-)tier programs in engineering and/

or agriculture)) a "Kinsey-like trove" of data regarding mainline and aberrant masturbatory practices, and, while many claimed to be impressed with his ability to elicit such seemingly forthcoming responses from his subjects, a recurring critique was that his analysis was, ultimately, "excessively Aristotelian" (by which the critic usually meant that it involved a robust system of categorization that nonetheless failed to provide any meaningful psychological or sociological insight).

Sensing this (as the rejections poured in (or sometimes never came at all)), Baskin pitched a longitudinal study on "pornographic exposure and its impact on the sexual attitudes and relational success(-es) of heterosexual Millennial men" to an interview committee at the University of Nebraska—Kearney, and, though some expressed reservations about his ability to either acquire grant funding or explain his work to students and associated parties (by which they usually meant parents and/or administrators), they were interested enough to offer him a tenure-track position. It soon became clear, however, that the school's tenure committee likely wasn't willing to wait the fifteen years Baskin believed to be necessary for delivering accurate, consequential results, and so, after his first year of teaching, he again shifted focus.

This time, he simply added a qualitative component to his primarily ethnographic methods. In addition to asking about the bare facts of a particular subject's masturbatory habits, he would also collect information about each subject's emotional state immediately prior to, during, and up to twenty-four hours after each masturbatory event, and, as the data came in, he discovered that, while many men reported some level of post-masturbation guilt or shame (depending (and fairly predictably based) on the specific material used, the activities/obligations neglected in the process, the location of ejaculation (e.g. workplace, home, hotel, etc.), the level of precaution taken (e.g. the use of browser add-ons, ad blockers, "Incognito" mode, etc.) to ensure secrecy, and c.), there was a larger-than-expected group for whom such feelings became nearly unbearable and led to both drastic action (e.g. one subject who kept an old desktop solely for the viewing of pornography, only he felt so bad after each session that he cut its VGA cable in half with a chef's knife (perhaps because, deep down, he was incapable of getting rid of the machine itself) and then had to buy a new one (at a computer repair store some 50 miles away) a few months later when the urge to indulge once again became too powerful to resist, and this happened at least five times over the course of two-and-a-half years, and there's a part of the interview where the subject asks Baskin (in agitation) if once every six months counts as an addiction (or if addiction is measured solely in frequency), and Baskin says nothing for a while before simply acknowledging that the conventions of social scientific research prevent him from offering a response) and the formation of various formalized sub-cultures (many of which established online message boards, weekly support groups, isolated, technology-free retreats, and other forms of ritualized interaction) dedicated to alleviating (or providing supportive commiseration with) said feelings. Of these subcultures, the one most interesting to Baskin called itself "The Hand-to-Hand Society," and their mission statement revolved around a belief that any shame resulting from an act of pornography-accompanied masturbation had its roots in the increasingly virtual nature of self-pleasure, and that, only by returning to the (largely pre-internet) manual roots of sexual self-exploration could these feelings be overcome. In support of these core beliefs, then, they argued that every masturbatory instance should involve some level of human contact as it related to the acquisition of stimulatory material. They advocated, for example, buying "erotic stimulants and/or masturbatory aids" at gas stations or book retailers or adult superstores and even published a semiannual brochure that featured a list of locations where said material might be acquired (ranked based on a series of twenty-five factors, including "décor," "ease of access," "overall privacy of location," "prices," "selection" (including a list of categories featuring various sex acts, body types, hair colors, etc.), "ethics" (essentially an assessment of the economic distribution practices (as far as they could be known) of the production companies most frequently stocked by a particular location), "level of employee 'condescension,' 'judgment,' 'discretion,'" and c.) and even offered suggestions for what to do after the acquired material had served its purpose (since many of the more secretive (and/or ashamed) members, newcomers in particular, wanted to be immediately rid of it post-ejaculation), which suggestions included an index of society-held donation bins (the nearest of which to Baskin was in Council Bluffs, and he once drove all the way down 80 in the service of the broader project and found it looked just like a standard dumpster (which, a subject later told him, was exactly the point)), a series of ideas for "re-gifting" (e.g. wrapping it up as though it were a Christmas present and leaving it atop your garbage can for the enjoyment of your local sanitation crew and/or alleyway scrapper), markets for potential re-sale, and methods for storage, collection, and subsequent organization. Privately, Baskin ascribed a level of "self-righteousness," to Hand-to-Hand members (though he never would have compromised the data by saying so out loud, even if he did repeatedly ask about the idea that paying for pornography was actually more ethically troubling than downloading it for free (given that there was no way to ensure (despite anyone's "best attempts") that one's money was going to the actresses, and, therefore, it was entirely possible that one was merely subsidizing the very worst parts of the industry), to which members usually responded with an argument about industry problems and consumer problems (the idea being that the customer's good-faith effort was more important than the concrete details of the financial trail), an argument Baskin understood without quite accepting (at least not personally)), though he did find their dedication admirable. Of course, his real respect was reserved for a number of them (a sub-subculture, as it were) who had, after (in some cases) years of using the Hand-to-Hand method, given up pornography altogether (sometimes out of exhaustion, sometimes out of a kind of last-straw paranoia (usually surrounding being caught or discovered), and sometimes out of a suddenly unignorable feeling of emptiness, a moment when the physical pleasure felt less pulsing or explosive than the sheer level of effort involved), and they each (in some form) told him that they'd done research on the neurochemical details of orgasm and found that each one was identical, no matter the external input, and any feeling of difference on the part of the subject was invented or socialized or both, and, once one realized this, it became clear that the best form of masturbation was that relying entirely on one's own brain (and hands (or other physical aids), of course). Although there were also moments (usually unstated), when these same subjects seemed unnerved (when they blinked too quickly or glanced around the room at the various stacks of adult magazines Baskin had gathered and organized in case they might become necessary) or unsure of themselves, and Baskin wondered if they'd actually succeeded in drowning out the reptilian brain, if they'd really found a way to be free from the cultural need to be stimulated in particular ways and by particularly pixelated versions of women, or if, deep down (or maybe right there on the surface) they missed their former rituals. If, given the chance, they'd go back to their darkened rooms and lotions and (boxes of) tissues in a heartbeat, even though they'd "evolved" and even though they had more time and (overall and indisputably, according to the data) better relational and physical health outcomes. Sometimes (usually at night and usually alone in his office (while conducting his own, individual research)), he thought they would. Then, he'd sit around (feeling a little ashamed himself) and wonder what this underlying desire might mean for hegemonic mankind, only to decide that he'd probably rather not know (or maybe that he already did).

That Nuclear Football

I woke up in some kind of scrubland emptiness and figured Tom missed the exit for Denver. There was nothing but soybeans and roadkill and cow shit all around. Rob gave me a look and said we were still in Nebraska, that Tom wanted to find one of them nuclear silos because about two weeks ago he had this dream about a missileer. Her name was Lisa or Louise or Lorraine. She had red hair. She looked like a cheerleader or 4-H girl and worked underground flipping switches and answering phones, and she was about the only thing between any of us and the apocalypse, us and radioactive decay. Good for her, I said, and Tom pulled over across from some fence that looked like it belonged in 1966. He checked his phone. Rob and I stared out the windshield. Rob said, whatever it is you're planning, I don't want nothing to do with it, but Tom popped the trunk and went around back and said we could stay in the car if we wanted, and this was one woman he didn't plan to share.

He leaned against the bumper for a while. We could feel the car sinking from the weight of his ass. Rob watched in the rearview, and I turned around to look through the back. We saw him holding a cheap novelty football and writing something in permanent ink. I bet it's a phone number, said Rob, but I was pretty sure it was some type of dirty joke. Then we felt the car come up and saw Tom walking toward the fence and knew he was going to throw the fucker and sat there panicking, trying to think up realistic fake names. I was thinking he'd gun it when he came back, but instead he just gripped the wheel and sighed like a furnace, or else this sort of broken A/C.

What the fuck are you doing, said Rob, and we were supposed to be a mile high. We were supposed to be eight beers deep. Tom didn't move. Didn't even look at him, and then Rob got out, and I made to follow and told him if we were gonna walk away we damn well better act the least bit cool.

I think we did. We only glanced back the once. Maybe twice. We walked and jogged casual and eventually found a gas station had to be like four miles away. We bought a couple of Dr. Peppers and asked ourselves what was that asshole's problem and how in the hell did he get to be our friend. We had no clue about the second part. The first we figured had something to do with Lisa. We thought it might have been about activism or surveillance, or else maybe just insanity, and maybe he was going to sit there forever, listening to wild prairie and waiting for the end of the world.

Aksarben

The pitch was pretty simple. Nebraska splits 60 percent of its electoral votes (3 of 5) by congressional district, and two of the districts (NE-1 and NE-3) are noncompetitive (meaning all Democratic votes therein are inefficiently distributed). NE-2, however, is a swing district, having been decided by some 6,000 votes last cycle (out of around 269,000) and 19,000 votes two cycles ago (out of around 262,000). According to the calculations of Frank Dent, a Democratic operative and lifelong Husker, it would take an influx of around 30,000 reliably Democratic voters to turn NE-2 from a "lean Republican" to a "lean [and maybe even a "solid"] Democrat." This would secure an additional electoral vote for the party's presidential candidates, as well as a House seat, and, though this may have appeared small to some, it was clear to him that (in a system such as ours, anyway) every vote mattered (in particular when one was dealing with one vote out of 270 (or 435) instead of one vote out of 780,454 (the total number of votes cast for President statewide last cycle)). Therefore, it seemed only natural that he should start a non-profit (and he had long arguments with himself about whether to apply for 501(c)(3) or 501(c)(4) status (ultimately going with the latter because it was more flexible and permissive)) and attempt to raise enough capital to facilitate the migration of some 30,000, solidly Democratic Huskers (though, later, this was amended to include registered Democrats (or even simply professed Democratic sympathizers) from any nationwide "strong" or "solid" Republican district (although the bulk of the research suggested that convincing someone to move across state lines (and to Nebraska in particular) wouldn't be worth the resources required to give the appeal a realistic chance of success)) to the Nebraska 2nd.

It wouldn't be just capital, of course. There would also have to be connections made with local employers (and he began with ConAgra and Mutual of Omaha (and continued with Creighton and UNO and MCC and other area schools)). Job placement services (and consultants) would have to be established and funded. Housing would need to be made available (although he imagined developers and realtors would be excited about the potential economic gains driven by such population growth), and improvements in infrastructure would have to be lobbied for and secured. The process would be onerous, but Dent was a rolodex guy, and his roots went deep into the party establishment, and he attended fundraising dinners and did a few strategic favors and got a line on the party's A-list, which, of course, included Warren Buffett and George Soros (or at least a couple of their mid-level staffers).

Their response was more intrigued (or maybe entertained) than interested. They wanted to know what he was going to call the operation (Aksarben, which was Nebraska spelled backwards and, also (as Buffett no doubt knew), the name of the old Omaha horse track). Who would he target (the educated at first (especially in Lancaster County) and then Hispanics (to whom he planned to offer an army of bought-and-paid-for immigration lawyers, as well as fee-free remittance services) and then Natives and disaffected whites (people cut from the ag sector, the guys in the slaughterhouses, the mechanics all up and down 80, etc.))? And just what the fuck was the payoff (given that it would take what? 100 mil to be feasible (to which Dent replied no more than 80 (and a good start would be 35)), not to mention the negative impact of such "self-sorting" on polarization and the corresponding overall health of political discourse (which Dent said had pretty much been entirely submarined by partisan gerrymandering anyway)), anyway?

The payoff, he said, wasn't just the extra vote. The extra seat (though he really thought that should be enough). It was, he said, just think what happens when this thing takes off. Because why stop at Nebraska? And why think we're capped at just one? His job was to read the electorate, and he said people were pissed enough that this was only a start. Imagine the same thing across the river, and we'll send busloads to Sioux City. We'll take out that Nazi from the Iowa 4th. We'll move them into Des Moines and Council Bluffs and Cedar Rapids (and that doesn't even consider what we could do in Kansas or Colorado), and then we'll just sit back and watch. We'll raise glasses. We'll smile and toast ourselves while the whole goddamn prairie turns Carolina blue.

Hawk's Nest Drive

The wife likes to drive around these subdivisions on the weekends. She's partial to the ones out near Offutt because they got reduced prices on account of the air traffic, and I always say to her, I say, "Hon, if it's a fantasy, you might as well dream big," but she likes the realism or the practicality I guess. Her favorite's this little group of cul-de-sacs they finished like two years ago, and when we first started coming it was like four houses. Used to be the only thing you could hear was blue jays and squirrels running through leaves, and now it's all these kids shouting and people must be my age wearing black socks and hand-washing their cars. All the streets are named after birds. One of them's called Chicken Hawk Circle. Another is Harrier Heights, and you get the general idea. Sometimes, we'll go to an open house, and the realtors must all get together and agree on a marketing strategy beforehand because we've heard the same story has to be six times already.

It starts back maybe ten years ago. There's only a dozen or so families living there, and one of them has this little Chihuahua name of Happy. They're on a walk one day, or maybe they just let Happy out to do her business, and whoosh, here comes some kind of hawk swooping in out of nowhere and taking the poor thing God knows where. They don't even bother to go looking for her because they're afraid of what they might find, and then there's a lot of screaming and crying and panicked phone calls to the neighbors. They go a little crazy for a while, and the realtor, who's sometimes a woman in her thirties with cans out to here and sometimes some greaser type looks like he'd be more natural down at the car lot, he always gets to this part and says something like who wouldn't? The tone becomes compassionate and sympathetic because the members of this family, they start yelling at people out on walks. Herding dogs inside and telling the owners about Happy over seven-layer bars and Nestle iced tea. They put up signs. The mother writes these letters to Hawkwatch International, and, swear to God, she must send one a day, and it gets bad enough that the organization starts to take note. Me and the wife are nodding along at this point. Sometimes, if she's feeling frisky, the wife'll ask what these letters say, and we'll get something like you can probably guess or ain't fit for Sunday company or let's just say she knows how to protect her cubs. Anyway, Hawkwatch writes her back, and the whole thing is like, I don't know, the Shakespeare of PR. We're so sorry, they say, and we can't bring little Happy back, but there's an affiliate over at UNO, and we've been in touch, and they're going to send someone out to do some banding or tagging or whatever you call it, and that'll help make sure this doesn't happen again. So, okay, she says. Doesn't think it'll do much good, but she's a Husker, and she's nothing if not polite. She plans to give the guy a piece of her mind, of course, and ask him why the hell they can't just shoot the thing down, most likely in an indirect way. It *is* the natural solution, after all, and she doesn't expect he'll have an answer, but she figures the mere act of asking will help. Except it doesn't. Because she doesn't even get to meet him, at least not really. The guy, whose name, funny enough, is Lincoln, shows up with his nets and coffee cans and bird bands, not to mention a few starved-looking grad students, and the first thing they see is a dead red-tailed hawk right there in the middle of this woman's driveway. It's gotta be pretty fresh because the husband was out there drinking coffee not 25 minutes before, and he didn't see a thing. The bird looks like it's been shot. Through the gut, maybe, or else her thick little neck. The whole neighborhood swears it heard nothing, and the woman looks too shocked to be guilty, and she gives one of the grad students three peanut butter sandwiches and a red and white tailgate cooler so they can take the bird back to the lab, which, of course, they do, but it's only out of courtesy, the realtor always says. Only because she insists. Because what's anyone going to do with a dead bird anyway? Ain't gonna eat it, and are you gonna perform an autopsy? Stuff it and sell it and hang it on some tavern wall? Find poor Happy? the wife says once, all hopeful, and that gets nothing but a sales laugh. A pity laugh, and this is usually when we look at each other as if we're going to walk away.

Then, the realtor gets all sincere. The point, he says, is it ain't just about the house. It's about the neighborhood. The camaraderie, and where else are you going to find someone willing to go to those lengths for you and yours? That's Midwest living, he says. The best America can offer right here on this very block, and at this point we always nod. We ask for a card. Then, we walk outside, and there's flags whipping in the wind and people on porches, and most of them cough and arch their eyebrows, or else they give us the side-eye on our way back to the car.

Pork Barrel Politics

Shift ends, and Eddie's in the parking lot telling me he stole a hog's head during one of the breaks. He says he's got it in this big red cooler his lady friend likes to use to pack his lunch. Thing has to weigh 12 pounds at least, and that's not including the cooler, and he's gonna put it in the trunk where the A/C can't get and drive on out to DC. He says he's got this plan to stick it on the front gate of the White House along with a sign about tariffs or ethanol or the goddamn EPA, and he needs an accomplice. He wants to take me with.

"Lincoln'd be better," I say, "On account the missus and all."

So, okay, fine, he says, and ain't like it matters much. Long as some senator or governor sees it and long as somebody's made to pay.

He bought his car used, and the last guy smoked through the seats, and on the way we talk about crop circles and roadkill and barns look more like rubble. Like them ruins you see on TV. It's one of them nights is all orange sunset and hot as hell, and I swear I can smell the cargo rotting away back there, but Eddie says that's only manure, or maybe Nebraska itself. He thinks we should have brought one for an insurance company. And also one for ConAgra too. About 20 miles out, he starts coughing, and you can tell he's having second thoughts, so I tell him, I say, "What's the difference between a politician and a space alien?" and Eddie lays on the horn and then sticks his arm out the window because this one's a real old favorite, and the punchline is something about how one of them's eager to probe, and the other just sits there in the corner. He's fil-

ing his nails. He's counting up votes, and all he can think about is
when will he get the chance to fuck.

Kansas City Blues

For the honeymoon, the bride's cousin (who worked for ADM) got them two nights at the Kansas City Marriott. He used his reward points. The room was on the tenth floor, and they spent most of their time doing things that were free. They rode the elevator up and down. They watched HBO. They walked past a million fountains and went to an art museum (where the groom made thrusting motions behind the naked statues, and the bride pretended to be in stitches (though she was really only mildly amused)).

On the second night, they did buy nosebleeds for the Royals. It rained on and off, and there was an hour-and-a-half delay, and the Indians led 9-1 when they left (sometime during the top of the 6th). They thought they'd beat the traffic, but then it ended up that they couldn't find the car. The parking lot was the size of Nebraska. Panic alarms kept going off at random intervals, and they didn't have keyless entry, and there was so much noise that it wouldn't have helped at all.

They were there for so long the game ended. The people walking by started to look familiar (like the woman with the neck tattoo, or the girl who couldn't have been more than 19 (not much younger than them, actually) and wore those pants that were practically leggings (and the bride kept wondering if the groom wanted to find her instead of the car)), and they realized they were all going in circles. The groom asked the bride why she never wrote anything down. Engines came to life in the background, and men (and maybe the groom was one of them) yelled "Fuck" as loud as they could. Finally, the bride stopped dead in Section C4 and sat herself down on the pavement. She looked up. The sky was starless (and you couldn't have seen them even if it were clear), and the groom braced himself for one of them feminine breakdowns, or else some kind of divorce right then and there.

"What the fuck, Delilah?" he said, and she smiled. She laid flat on her back. She offered him her hand (and he thought, if he accepted, it would probably be with his shoe) and said, "Listen. If we stay where we are, it won't be long till it's empty. Till the whole world ends, and won't that be grand? You and me will be the only ones here."

Shit From Shimerda

With his (Democratic) candidate down 10 points in September, Frank Dent made an ad. He never bought airtime. Just sent the file to a few close friends (who happened to make money selling products through various social media platforms) and waited for things (and people) to click.

The ad itself was inspired by (or maybe, as some Republican strategists and operatives argued, an essential shot-for-shot copy of) something McConnell did in '84, when he was running against this asshole named Huddleston. Maybe you know it. It features a gang of bloodhounds (not to mention some redneck in flannel) running around looking for the Democrat (on account of he's missed some big Senate votes), who, it turns out, is in Puerto Rico, sitting by a pool and getting paid to deliver a speech. Only real difference is, in Dent's ad, the bloodhounds are Irish setters, and they're looking for Ben Sasse, and, at some point, the setters meet someone dressed like Willa Cather, and she says, "Ol' Sasse don't know shit from Shimerda" and then runs off to thresh some hay or else plough a road through wild frontier, and, believe it or not, the thing took off.

First there were the memes, and then the cable news morning shows got ahold of it (and aired explanatory segments punctuated by cackling laughter), and they bleeped the "shit" but played the ad often enough it may as well have paid freight. People started discussion groups. *My Ántonia* sold more copies on Amazon than any other book (though still trailed most movies and baby accessories and household goods), at least in the Midwest. Dent went on

CNN and then had these wild dreams of revolution, about being the man who flipped the switch, the guy who turned the die-hard prairie blue as the Pacific. Blue as California sky. Polls into October showed the race within the margin of error, and one of them even had his candidate (who was deep into a second round of bowling alley and VFW tours) ahead.

Then, the blowback started. Fox brought on a few strategists, and Dent's counterpart (who wore sneakers and conducted live focus groups) said most people found the ad's elitism downright offensive. "Leave it to the Democrats," said Newt Gingrich, "to release an ad that requires annotations." Someone even leaked an internal campaign proposal that had the Democrat reading aloud from *My Ántonia* on the steps of the capitol in the name of public education, and Sasse himself said it would be better if he read it out on the steps of the Nebraska Union over at UNL because you just knew he wanted to smoke a bowl and play hacky-sack in between chapters (to which the Democrat said it'd be better to smoke between books (given that there were something like 80 chapters, and smoking that much would be "deliberately unpleasant," would give anyone a hacking cough), and for a while this spawned its own set of memes (most of which featured the candidate as a sort of cross between Jeff Bridges (in *Big Lebowski* regalia) and the Marlboro Man), and it probably would have won the day were it not for a concerted effort on behalf of various Evangelical groups, most of which argued that casual jokes about drug use were what really demonstrated a fundamental misunderstanding of Cather, who ("as most Christians recognize") was a true Nebraska heroine (and also espoused a kind of Gospel of hard work and sacrifice and compassion that was fundamental to the religious fabric of the real America (by which they meant mostly the middle (mostly white) portion))), and all of this added up to a kind of political stalemate, though, as election night went on (and Dent found himself gathered at the Omaha Livestock Exchange (where the elevators made rustic noises that the dozens of vegans present claimed were the millions of ghosts of slaughtered cattle) with the rest of the campaign), the race was too close to call. Sasse would be up by 1200 votes, and then it would be 481 the other way, and if the state had a collective consciousness, what it would have thought was this. That, whatever happens, this has been a blast (and maybe even worth the sheer boiling rage (pretty much exactly) half of us will feel when it's all said and done), and next time (and the time after that (and the one after that)) we can get all wound up and confident that we're doing it right, that we've got this whole politics thing pretty damn well figured out.

Them Racket Boys

After the Huskers lost, me and Adler went down to the football field. We stood under the goalposts. We drank Windsor. It was 24 degrees, and I had on this old stocking cap, but he wasn't wearing a whole lot beyond what you would call the liquid coat. I said, hey, it was always coming down the pike, and he looked up at the stars and told me this wasn't about football, and the last twenty years were like listening to a baby have a bad dream. I said, don't I know it, and then we talked about computers and women and this friend we had, this guy Matt, who got real drunk one night and decided to move to Omaha and then killed this cop out there for what they said was fun, for no goddamn reason at all. Truth is, we always knew the sonofabitch had a hair-trigger. They'd given him the needle the day before, and Adler said we should get revenge. Thought we might break some glass all up and down the sidelines and then hope the state police show up and see where it goes from there. I figured it was maybe better to just plant one of them crosses like they got out on the highways at the 50-yard line and then hold some kind of vigil all the way through the whole rest of the night. Like we should just sit there and share a bottle and maybe hope some crows come by we can shoot with a pellet gun, and so that ended up being exactly what we did. Minus the cross. And we didn't see no crows. Only heard a couple up by the field lights, and Adler said they sounded like they were speaking Mexican, or maybe in Morse code, and so he sent me out to get another bottle thinking maybe that might help us understand. When I came back, I found him face down in the end zone and had to shake him twice just to get him to roll over. I gave him my hat. Put my hands over his face. I said his nose was looking awful red, and we better get back to the car or else they might have to cut it off. He smiled like a playing card, like the king of fucking hearts. He told me, he said, if I had to make a prediction I'd say there's no one's gonna come and claim the body, and Mattie's gonna be buried in a prison cemetery, and even if there is such a thing as heaven, nothing is ever gonna be the same again.

Alliance

At Carhenge, Mike said we needed to talk. It was winter, and we were the only ones there. Icicles dripped from the bumpers of old Cadillacs. We stood under them like they were mistletoe, or else rockets, hoping to launch themselves down below. He said he never told me this, but back when he was flunking out of Lincoln he used to sell plasma twice a week, and sometimes, on the same day, he'd go ahead and donate sperm too. This is back when he was still eligible. Back when they didn't ask so many questions, or maybe he just fed them a whole lot of lies. He'd use the money to buy a fifth of Windsor and share it with his roommates, and they had a name for this. It was called the Triple Crown. They always finished the bottle, and it was three of them in total, and he'd usually outdrink the other two combined.

On those nights, he'd have these dreams, these visions, hallucinations while passed out on the floor. He saw armies of children coming to his house. His wife hid in the basement. The kids were all male, and they looked 15 or 19 or, on occasion, 32. They had tattoos of hawks and scars on their forearms, and they asked for the things he would have asked for, which meant beer and money for women, or else any place soft where they might be allowed to crash. His wife would stomp her feet and shake her head no, but she couldn't talk or maybe he couldn't hear, and he'd find himself helpless, torn between obligations and basically frozen in place. He said the whole thing was always more prophecy than dream, and he took my hand and asked me if I could do it. If he could consider me in. His fingers felt like wet cement, and I told him I'd have to think about it. Even though I'd already made up my mind.

Interloping

A few years back, I published a collection of short fiction. It was called *48 Blitz*, and most of the stories were about football. I'd go to these colleges in the middle of nowhere and read about kids crashing into each other. Kids getting yelled at. Kids locking arms or jumping around or crying at the west end of the field.

Most of the time, the audience was well-meaning. In Kearney, they drove through a rainstorm. They wore jeans and Husker hats and acted like they were in on the joke. I sold two books and talked to a kid who said he played for the Lopers. He mentioned spring practice and bad knees and a coach who still called him Gary, even though his name was Steve. He had a copy of the book. There were drawings in the margins. Little wolf heads he glanced at while asking if I thought he was wasting his time. I did, but I told him the game could still be beautiful. I said I didn't want to discourage anyone. That the choice is always yours, and every man makes his own decisions, and I'd never dream of telling anyone what he should do.

Luisa

She was my cousin, and I was in love with her. In the past, I might have qualified that sentence. I might have offered that I was too young to know about common decency and the rules of family life, or that I probably didn't know too much about what love actually was, or that she was the only girl I'd ever spoken to, which made her a natural target for the gathering storm of adult emotions. No more, however. I'm at peace with it. I was in love with my cousin, and you would have been too.

Her red hair fell perfectly, even just out of bed, and when she went about her chores, collecting the milk and feeding the chickens, there was this harmonious correspondence between the motions of her long arms and the look in her blue eyes. When one of the hens needed to be slaughtered, we'd send Luisa to take her out to the wooden table by the shed. If I would have been older, I might have imagined her as a kind of benevolent escort, an Angel of Death who gave every victim a martyr's courage, quietly assuring each of them that they were doing something worthwhile and transcendent and that they'd be rewarded and happy and that it wouldn't hurt much anyway. At the time, however, I went along with my gruff Uncle Jake.

"Look at that," he said once as he watched a hen being carried toward the shed. "We should give her a pack of cigs next time and maybe a special kind of feed." He laughed after that, and I remember thinking about Luisa more as executioner than angel, which is one of the things I regret.

Uncle Jake was all she had. He was my mother's brother, and, when his wife left, she invited them to come live with us. As long as they helped out, they'd always be welcome, was what Mother said. He was different from my dad. Louder, mostly. Always filling silences with these odd comparisons that functioned as jokes. "Got enough shit on these boots to fertilize the goddamn Sahara," was his main line. He'd never been a farmer, but he had the personality for it. Hardworking, certainly, which is why Mother tolerated his occasional vulgarity. When he swore, she'd look at me and say, "Anthony, you listen to your uncle. But if I ever catch you talking like him, it'll be the last time you're able to speak without a stutter." In our family, Dad was the soft one. He spent long days in the field, and when he came home he was always too exhausted to do any kind of intense discipline. It was Mother you didn't want to cross.

She was most relaxed at night, after dinner, when we'd all sit in front of this old stone fireplace, sometimes wrapped in quilts that Luisa helped sew. We didn't have a television. At some point when I was really small, we all started keeping dream journals. It was how we entertained ourselves. Mother would make chamomile tea because coffee was reserved for getting through chores. Dad never shared what he wrote, so he became our leader.

"Anyone got a good one tonight?' he'd start, and if no one responded, he'd just choose. "Jake?" he might say.

My uncle had wild dreams. I remember sometimes he'd say, "Huh, well, you know there, Dan, I'm not sure that'd be a good one to share right now. Least not until little Tony over there's about 15, hey T?" He'd laugh, and I remember hating him for not using my full name. Dad would smile nervously, and Mother would give Uncle Jake a stern look. You knew she meant it when she set down her knitting.

Other times, though, he'd use his dreams to tell stories, and they'd often be ghostly ones, haunted by dead pastors or old farmer's wives. Those nights were the best. Luisa would move closer to me on the floor, and sometimes we'd share a quilt and she'd grab my arm when Uncle Jake reached a particularly frightening point.

I remember thinking it meant she liked me since she was a couple years older, probably fourteen, and I thought maybe she was faking her fear. When Mother would teach us lessons in the afternoon, she always seemed too smart to be fooled by ghosts and creatures of the night. It felt good to think that maybe she just wanted to get closer to me, that I was more important than all those chickens. I could actually understand the meaning of her fingers pressing into my bony arms.

I shared a dream once where I had died, and there were these two men in shiny, metallic suits standing over a pile of bones that I somehow knew was me. And they were dusting them off with these brushes like archeologists, as if I were some kind of dinosaur or exotic species. At one point, one of them stopped dusting and removed one of my upper arm bones. He turned to his partner and said, "I think you ought to take a look at this."

"What have you got there?" said the partner.

"It looks like a fingerprint," replied the other one.

"Indeed it does," said the partner, and the two of them put it in a case and brought it with them, leaving the rest of me behind in what looked like our shed. Mother thought the dream was creepy, but Uncle Jake said it reminded him of these books he used to read and so he liked it. I didn't tell them, but that fingerprint was from Luisa. It was hers, and that night it felt like she snuggled up extra close and I didn't care what anyone thought of the dream, so long as she would just stay right there and not move for a good long time.

If I remember right, all the trouble started the next day. Dad and Uncle Jake and a few neighbors were out in the field putting up a hoop house because Mother wanted a bigger garden. Luisa and I sat next to each other at the kitchen table working on lessons. Our kitchen was small, a series of floral prints recurring on the white linoleum floor. Mother had a roast going in the slow cooker on the counter. When I looked up from my math worksheet, I could see condensation gathering on the inside of the lid and hear a tiny rattling hiss. It sounded like Morse code, like something inside was trying to get out. Mother was explaining infinity to Luisa.

"It's everything," she said, "It's numbers going on forever."

Luisa didn't understand. "It can't just keep going. It has to end sometime."

"Maybe this bit in the book will help." Mother read, "Imagine that you are counting. You get to 10 then 100 then, eventually, 1,000,000. You spend your whole life counting, every day, every minute. There is always another number. You could keep counting forever and ever and never start back at zero." Mother added, "That's infinity."

"So, does that mean you're not really counting at all?" Luisa stared at the slow cooker, her mouth parted slightly. I fought back a powerful urge to hug her.

"What do you mean, sweetheart?"

"If there is no end, then aren't you always at the beginning? If it just keeps going, then how do you ever know where you are?" The rattle seemed louder, and she looked ready to cry. I couldn't stop myself.

"Maybe it's like our dreams," I blurted, dropping my pencil and inching my left hand closer to Luisa. The air between us felt magnetized, electric but impenetrable.

"Anthony," Mother said, "Is your worksheet finished?" Luisa looked down at my hand, then slowly panned up. As her red hair brought out the blue of her eyes, I found the courage that only primary colors can inspire.

"No, Mother, listen," I said, "When Dad asks Uncle Jake about his dreams, we never know what he might say. He could say anything. If we had to guess his dream before he told us, we'd never get it right."

"I don't see how that helps," said Mother, but I could see understanding making its way across Luisa's face.

"It's like infinity. We don't know the beginning or the end, but we can still like the story while we're hearing it."

"And he never runs out of stories," said Luisa.

Mother walked over to the slow cooker. She removed the lid and made a fanning motion with her hand before gently replacing it. "Thank you, Anthony. Does that help, sweetheart?"

"Yes," replied Luisa softly, and she looked at me and gave a sad sort of smile and I could see her lips moving and they said "thank you" and I don't think to this day I've ever felt happier.

That night, when we gathered under our blankets and sipped our tea, Dad began like he always did.

"Anyone got a good one tonight?" There was a long pause, and he looked at me and then at Uncle Jake, silently asking one of us to volunteer. Next to me, Luisa shifted, her thigh no longer pressing against mine.

"I do," she whispered, so quietly that I still wonder how he heard her.

"Please," said Dad, his eyes darting around the room. Mother's knitting ceased, and Uncle Jake's perpetual half-smile receded, transforming itself into a worried look. It was rare for Luisa to share dreams, and, when she did, her eyes would glaze over and she'd look lost and reflective and none of us would have any idea where she was.

"Ah, well," my uncle said, "I've got a coupla good ones too, hon. Maybe you could save yours for another time. Not like we won't be back at it again tomorrow."

"I want to do it, Dad. I can do it." It was the first time I'd ever heard her call him Dad. Her voice was quiet but somehow forceful. Uncle Jake gave a slow nod.

"Alright then. Guess mine can just as easily be saved for another night too. You go ahead, little lady. I'm glad to listen."

"Thank you," she said, and the room became silent. I heard the wooden floorboards creaking from our weight, a sound that always made me shiver. Pulling the blanket up, I leaned into Luisa, close enough that our shirts were touching. Fabric ruffled and brushed the skin underneath.

"I was in a cornfield," she began, "Just me. Alone. The corn was tall, up to my chest. It must have been summer. I don't remember being warm even though I was wearing a long dress. Like the ones you have, Aunt Edith."

Mother nodded. I drew my arms into my body underneath the blanket. The way she said Mother's name was magic.

"It was close to sunset, and I was dancing. I don't know why. But there was music coming from every stalk. And I would spin in place and my dress would flutter, and after every turn I would be in a different part of the field. It was like I was flying, only without my feet leaving the ground."

She stopped, looking past Dad and Uncle Jake and into the fireplace. I thought about the pink of the sunset combining with the red of her hair and the little smile she'd give as her feet twirled in place. I thought about being there too. I thought about putting my arm around her in between the stalks.

"The field was the whole world," she continued, "I knew that somehow. It just went on and on forever, the rows and the stalks. And I could keep spinning and ending up in different places, but there would always be corn. And I would always be dancing. And it would always be just me."

She kept staring straight ahead, and they all thought there would be more. I wanted to tell her not to worry, that I'd find her somewhere in that field, that we'd be together and happy, and dancing is better with a partner, but I couldn't. I could only reach under the blanket and try to find her arm. Her shirt was softer than mine. It was a sweater, wool and knitted by Mother. I traced the groves in the fabric down toward her fingers, cupping my hand like I was holding a bird or petting a dog. When I hit skin, I stopped. I didn't grab or push. I just let my hand sit there, touching hers, telling her everything I always wanted to say with my palm instead of my tongue. My palm said, "You are not alone. I am with you. Let me stay. Please?"

Something changed in her after that. Her gentle way began slowly transforming into something darker, something more sinister. Now, I would call it depression. Then, I just thought maybe she was as hopelessly in love as I was. Sometimes, we'd be assigned to feed the chickens together, or to tag along and help with the milking. The thought of being with Luisa made getting up at five in the morning more than tolerable. Her face would be in my dreams and it would say "thank you" and her fingers would be touching my elbow. Then they'd slowly make their way up toward my cheek and I'd feel warm and search for her eyes. Sometimes, I'd touch her hair just before I woke up, and there would be this moment of utter sadness at having seen the image evaporate. Then, I'd remember where I was and where I was going and look forward to seeing her face next to me at the barn or feeling her hand brush mine as we walked from the shed to the coop carrying small bags of chicken feed. We barely spoke. She barely smiled. We were in love, I knew, but I think I just assumed that it was supposed to be sad. I began to look at the days as supplying the raw material for my dreams, these snippets of Luisa far off and distant that would turn into caresses and confessions under the cover of sleep.

On the last day we were paired up for chores, Uncle Jake found us with the chickens.

"Great news, Tony boy," he said, "Your ma's got it into her head to cook us up some fried bird tonight. Mashed potatoes and everything. How'd you two feel about picking out one of those little ladies and bringing her out to the shed. Your dad and I will take care of the rest." He winked at Luisa as he strolled away, whistling. The two of us stood there for a while, not moving.

"Do you want to pick?" I remember asking, looking down at the floor for fear of what would happen if our eyes met.

"No. No," she said, "I can't. It's too much knowing what's going to happen."

"Do you want *me* to then?"

She just nodded, and I thought I could see something clouding in her eyes as she closed them, unable to watch what was about to take place. I hesitated for a long time, trying to avoid every set of eyes in the coop.

"Did I ever tell you about my mom?" Luisa said suddenly, her voice cracking somewhere in the middle.

"No."

"Don't tell my dad, but I remember her. He tries really hard to be happy. He thinks it makes me happy. Sometimes, he's right."

"Oh."

"He thinks I blame myself, but I don't. And I don't blame him either." The hens huddled together, pecking. "I didn't know how she felt until you talked to me at the table. It wasn't about math. That's why I said thank you. You were right, you know. About infinity."

"I was?" There was a plump brown hen, right in the middle of the group.

"It's so open, so freeing. Not like here. That must have been what she felt like." When I reached for the hen, the others scattered. In my arms, she squirmed.

"Don't worry," said Luisa, "You're getting out."

We walked toward the shed, where Dad and Uncle Jake waited. Luisa whispered to the hen, looking her directly in the eyes. They were both so calm. She was close to my arms as she was speaking, and I felt her breath even through a light jacket and long sleeves. Dad had a small knife in his hand, and Uncle Jake was holding a milk carton, its bottom cut out and the top widened. Between them was a white five-gallon bucket.

Uncle Jake put the plastic carton around the hen and took her from me, holding onto her feet. Luisa continued whispering and there was little resistance. He held the chicken upside down, and Dad grabbed its beak and pulled until it was directly over the bucket. Luisa grabbed my hand.

"We should stay," she said, "It'll be easier for her that way." I nodded, biting my lip.

Dad took the knife, maybe three or four inches long, and pressed it lightly against the hen's neck. With a small pulling motion, he broke through, and blood began to fill the bucket. It came out calmly, in a stream no wider than the trickle of a hose. Its dark red color made Luisa's hair look pink and fresh. Dad put the knife inside the hen's mouth and poked it through the top of her beak. She began to twitch in Uncle Jake's arms, but he wasn't about to let go.

"I tell ya, the little lady's still got some fight left in her," he said, "Tough little cookie this one." Luisa flinched, fingers suddenly resting against my wrist. Dad must have seen me crying.

"Don't worry, Anthony. She didn't feel anything."

The only thing I felt was Luisa's hand squeezing mine. It was only barely, with just a little pressure from both her thumb and forefinger. It was a prayer, I thought, and I asked God to help me remember what it felt like.

———

That night was the last time I dreamt. She was there, as she had been nearly every night. We were in the coop, sitting on the ground. There were bits of feed scattered everywhere, but the chickens were gone.

"Where did they go?" I asked.

"Home."

"But this is their home."

"No. It's just where they stay."

"Oh."

"Their home is somewhere else. Somewhere you don't know about."

"Do you know where it is?"

"No," she replied, "But I'm going to find out someday."

When she said it, she stood up, dashing out of the coop and into the night. I followed as quickly as I could, watching her hair flip back toward me from under a green stocking cap. The strands collected into motion lines, pulling her into some future I needed to be part of. When she reached the shed, she opened the door slowly, turning around as she entered and motioning for me to follow. Her wave was perfect and elegant, flowing like the hem of a long dress. In my excitement, I stumbled, and by the time I reached the door, she was already inside.

The shed was pitch black, and it was impossible to see. I tripped and groped and shouted her name at least three times, but there was never any response. There was the sense of panic you get in dreams, where you're disoriented and lost, trapped in a space that feels so familiarly uncharted. Running from it, I exited. Outside, there was our table, same as in reality, made of plywood and leaning against the shed wall. On it, in a neat little pile, was a set of chicken bones, looking sharp and menacing, shining under a half moon and a distant set of stars.

The next morning, Luisa was gone. Mother was at the kitchen table crying. I could hear Dad and Uncle Jake outside talking, and Dad was saying something about looking around town, and he was sure she'd be somewhere. She couldn't have gotten far. Uncle Jake wasn't saying anything, but I heard the truck start up and Mother blew her nose and asked about breakfast. No thank you, I wasn't hungry, but what happened? And she said I shouldn't worry, but I did. I knew that I'd dreamed her away somehow, that I was the one who'd helped her finally understand. It was that stupid worksheet and maybe I should have listened to Mother in the first place and then the whole sorry episode could have been avoided.

Still, I thought she'd come back. I thought Dad and Uncle Jake would open the door sometime that afternoon, and there she'd be, talking about sleepwalking or getting lost or some other logical explanation. When they didn't return until late at night, and I heard the truck leaving again early the next morning, the reality of it became clear. Luisa was gone.

Uncle Jake made it worse. His eyes became forever misty and distant, and the one-liners disappeared completely. He started calling me "Anthony," and whenever I gave him a playful elbow to try and revive some of his old energy, he'd just reach down and pat my head softly, with the exact same amount of pressure Luisa had always used on my arm.

Sometime that summer, we tried to start dream sharing again, and I resorted to a fake journal that I filled with stories of bumper crops and winning lottery tickets. Not even that could dull the pain. Mother had attempted to turn it into a healing session, instructing Dad to ask each of us, "What did Luisa bring you?" before we shared. It was supposed to be therapeutic. Like we were turning her into an angel, always remembering who she was and what she meant. It ended up making it worse. Uncle Jake went along for a while, and we could tell he was trying, but he could never make it through without breaking down. His stories disappeared with Luisa, and, when he left six months later, his brown hair had turned gray at the edges and his scratchy, forceful voice had deteriorated into a meek whisper.

He moved into town and started working at the slaughterhouse, cutting and slicing over and over in this way that kept his mind from ever wandering too far from the task. We heard from him only rarely, in Christmas letters filled with hollow, forced cheerfulness and vague references to "work buddies" and "the bachelor life." We missed the help at the farm, and I remember long days with Dad, taking care of the cows and the corn. I haven't touched a chicken since. Can't even eat it anymore, though Mother made me choke it down all the way up until the day she died. Somehow, we made it through, but it was never the same. Luisa had been a quiet, comforting presence, this vulnerable beauty whose gentleness was peace itself. Without her, there were no more nights around the fireplace, no more stolen touches underneath home-sewn quilts, and, worst of all, no more dreams. I barely even sleep anymore, and though any farm provides enough work to keep your mind occupied, I've never been able to shake the feeling of emptiness, this idea that if I'd only done something different, she'd still be here.

Mother hung on long after Dad, but when she finally passed about a year ago, I sold the land and came here. I keep thinking I'll run into Luisa one day. Maybe at the grocery store. It's the only place I ever go. Otherwise, it's just here, this apartment, a sparsely furnished one-bedroom that somehow still manages to raise up echoes of her constantly, all the time and every day. The bookshelf in the corner is filled with black composition notebooks, and they spill off the wood and onto the floor, collecting there like cockroaches, only they don't scatter when you turn on the lights. She's in every single one of them, but the words never seem to come out right. It's like she can't be captured, can't be understood. Like she really was something otherworldly, something ghostly and angelic. I keep thinking, if I try hard enough, maybe I can dream her back. I've turned my waking life into a dream, and maybe if I stay at it long enough, she'll wander into it someday, and we'll look at each other, middle-aged and lonely, and sit on the floor in silence, with her gripping my arm just above the elbow. If I continue forever, writing on and on and into the infinite future, she'll have to show up eventually. In the meantime, all that's left is this story, and the next one, and whatever it is that happens after that.

Acknowledgments

Thank you to so many people. Mom, you're the best reader I know. Thank you for always sharing your love of history and words and stories with me and for all your incredible feedback on this book. Dad, I am always so impressed by your curiosity about people and places, and nobody, and I mean nobody, tells stories like you. Thank you for always sharing them. Maria, your hard work is an inspiration. Thanks for teaching me what it means to really focus on completing a project.

Meg, I don't know how anything is possible without your support. Your thoroughness as a reader and your ability to teach me how to be honest and forthright and compassionate has always been unparalleled. I love you. Thank you. Eliza, thanks for teaching me how to laugh and be awed by the world. I hope you always will be. Russ and Mary, thanks for all the wonderful conversation and support, but also thanks for your dining room table. Some of my favorite stories in this collection were written there.

To Pedro Ramírez, the attention you gave to these stories was just, well, it was awe-inspiring. You read this collection in that way that all authors want their books to be read, and I am so grateful for your insights on everything from content to ordering to line-by-line alterations. Indeed, Split/Lip's support of this book has been obvious from the very beginning. I owe a major debt of gratitude to Kristine Langley Mahler. Your willingness to shepherd me through this whole process is something I won't ever forget, and your editorial insights were invaluable. Thank you for your words, your support, and your basic decency and devotion. To Caleb Tankersley, you helped me navigate some of the parts of publishing a person doesn't really think about until the book is ready to come out, and I could not have done it without you. To David Wojciechowski, thank you for all your effort on the cover, for your willingness to listen, and for your promptness and professionalism. To all of you, I am so, so proud this is a Split/Lip book.

Thanks, also, to all my teachers, especially Cindy Scudiero, Scott Richardson, and Geoff Herbach. All of you inspired a passion for writing, and Geoff, every day I remember something else that you taught me. Your mentorship means a great deal to me.

Finally, I want to gratefully acknowledge the following publications, all of whom published versions of some of the stories found within this collection:

2 Bridges ("Brand New Man"), *Arcturus* ("Luisa"), *Bridge Eight* ("The Computer Wore Tennis Shoes"), *Chautauqua* ("Warriors"), *Crab Creek Review* ("Till Death"), *Dime Show Review* ("A Rising Tide"), *Great River Review* ("Penance"), *The Fourth River* ("Lincoln Highway Jesus"), *Hypertext* ("The Little Boy" (originally published as "Eulogy for David Vang, 1993-1997")), *Jabberwock Review* ("Happy Fish Bait n' Tackle"), *LandLocked* ("A Simple Explanation of Benefits"), *Marathon Literary Review* ("Power Left"), *The Masters Review* ("Big Red Nation"), *minnesota review* ("The Patron of the Prairie"), *Miracle Monocle* ("Message to the Grassroots"), *Levee Magazine* ("Roadside America"), *Nixes Mate Review* ("Alliance"), *Rock & Sling* ("Dissent"), *Salt Hill* ("Dawson County Postcards"), *Sip Cup* ("Spirit Guide"), and *The William & Mary Review* ("The Messenger").

About the Author

Brett Biebel's (mostly very) short fiction has appeared in dozens of print and online outlets, including *SmokeLong Quarterly*, *Emrys Journal*, *Chautauqua*, *Crab Creek Review*, *Salt Hill*, and *Third Point Press*. He holds an MA in Communication Studies from the University of Minnesota and an MFA in Creative Writing from Minnesota State University in Mankato. He has taught writing and speech courses at colleges and universities across the Midwest and South, and *48 Blitz* is his debut story collection. He lives in Iowa with his wife, Meg, and daughter, Eliza.

Now Available From

Split/Lip Press

 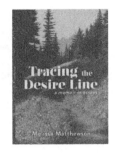

For more info about the press and our titles, visit

www.splitlippress.com

Follow us on Twitter and Instagram: @splitlippress

Made in the USA
Monee, IL
07 November 2020

46920151R00089